No More Nice

Amy MacDonald

Pictures by Cat Bowman Smith

A Sunburst Book
Farrar Straus Giroux

Text copyright © 1996 by Amy MacDonald
Pictures copyright © 1996 by Cat Bowman Smith
All rights reserved
Distributed in Canada by Douglas & McIntyre Ltd.
Printed in the United States of America
First published by Orchard Books, 1996
Sunburst edition, 2005
10   9   8   7   6   5   4   3   2   1

www.fsgkidsbooks.com

Library of Congress Cataloging-in-Publication Data
MacDonald, Amy.
    No more nice / by Amy MacDonald ; illustrated by Cat
Bowman Smith.
        p. cm.
    Summary: Eleven-year-old Simon has been raised to be
extremely well-behaved, but when he goes to visit his
unconventional great-aunt he discovers that not everyone
has the same ideas about good manners.
    ISBN-13: 978-0-374-45511-8 (pbk.)
    ISBN-10: 0-374-45511-2 (pbk.)
    [1. Behavior—Fiction. 2. Great-aunts—Fiction.
3. Individuality—Fiction.] I. Smith, Cat Bowman, ill.
II. Title.

PZ7.M1463No   1966
[Fic]—dc20
                                        96-7661

For Mary Wright MacDonald

Sort of . . . You Know

Where was Aunt Matilda?

Simon Maxwell stepped off the train and scanned the empty station parking lot. I must be late, he thought nervously. She must have gotten tired of waiting and gone home.

And though he'd never met his great-aunt, he imagined how cross she would look—her bony hands twitching, her black eyes flashing—as Simon apologized for making her drive to the station twice.

"I'm very sorry, Aunt Matilda," he would say, even though it wasn't his fault that the train was late.

And then she'd say, grumpily, "Humph, well, nothing to be done about it. What's done is done."

The reason Simon was not looking forward to meeting his great-aunt Matilda was that he knew very little about her. And the few things he did know about her had him worried. He knew she was very old. And he knew that the older people got, the grouchier and crankier they got, and the less they liked children. And Aunt Matilda hadn't even wanted him to come and stay in the first place—that much he knew for sure. Simon had been told all his life that it was rude to invite yourself to someone else's house—but that's exactly what his parents had done. They'd called up Aunt Matilda and "invited" Simon to go stay with her and Uncle Philbert. Some vacation this was going to be!

Simon dragged his suitcase over to a bench and sat down. He watched a spider trapping a fly in its web while he tried to think what he might do if no one at all came to pick him up. This pleasant daydream was interrupted by the scrape of tires on gravel.

An ancient black car pulled into the station in a cloud of dust. The door opened and a woman heaved herself out. She had piles of white hair that seemed intent on es-

caping from the weight of an enormous hat with purple feathers. Her eyes drooped at the corners and were not black (as he had imagined) but emerald. And she was not tall and bony, but small, rounded, and padded like a comfortable armchair.

"You're Simon," she said, puffing, "and I'm late." Simon stuck out his hand politely, but the woman surrounded him in a hug that smelled of lavender and licorice. "So, Simon Maxwell," she said, releasing him halfway, "how does your corporosity seem to gashiate?"

"Excuse me?" said Simon.

"Your corporosity," said the woman. "Is it gashiating nicely?"

Since Simon couldn't answer this curious question, he asked meekly, "Are you Aunt Matilda?"

"Of course I am, child!" she said. "I did not introduce myself because it's much more fun to try to guess who everybody is. And please call me Mattie. Everyone does. Have you been waiting long?"

Simon hesitated. He couldn't lie. But if he told the truth, it might sound rude, as if he was cross at Aunt Matilda—Aunt Mattie—for being so late.

"Only twenty minutes," he said at last, struggling as usual to be both truthful and polite.

"Oh, good," said Aunt Mattie. "I always try to be at least fifteen minutes late."

If Simon was surprised at this remark, he didn't have time to show it. His aunt swept him into the dilapidated car, first removing a large goldfish bowl from the front seat. Water sloshed over the sides, and the startled fish swam in frantic circles. "Don't you just *hate* goldfish?" She sighed. Simon, who had two goldfish of his own for pets, kept silent. "Someone gave these to me and so I do my best to make their lives interesting. They must get so *bored* in that bowl. Same old view, day after day. I'm taking them for a drive today. A change of scenery will cheer them up, don't you agree?"

The car finally started on the third try, and they lurched from the parking lot. Simon buckled his seat belt and looked over at his great-aunt curiously. This wasn't easy to do, since a potted ivy plant hung from the roof of the car, swaying between them. Simon wanted to tell Aunt Mattie he agreed with her about goldfish. But he felt somehow that would be unfair to his other aunt, Aunt Bea, who had given the fish to him for his birthday. After all, goldfish were better than no pets at all, sort of. And Simon's mother had never allowed him to have other pets, because, she said, they made too much mess, and think of the fleas and the germs, and Simon would never take care of them, and who would look after them

when the family went on trips, and, and, and . . . Well, she had a million reasons.

But instead of explaining any of this to his great-aunt, Simon simply said, "Yes, Aunt Mattie."

He gripped the door handle as the car careened over the road at a terrific speed. His aunt, though broad, was quite short, and her head just barely peeped above the steering wheel. It was hard to imagine that she could see over it at all.

"Now then," she said briskly, "tell me truly, do I look the way you thought I would? Hmm? Be honest."

But Simon couldn't. He just couldn't find a polite way to say, "You're fatter than I imagined." Or maybe, "I thought you would be skinny, like a witch." Or, "You are even older than I thought." If there was one thing his parents had taught him, it was that it was rude to make "personal" comments about people. You mustn't say they were fat or thin or had dimples or didn't have dimples or were hairy or bald or anything—even if it was true.

Grown-ups, he had noticed, always seemed to feel that it was perfectly okay for *them* to make personal comments about children. Most of his parents' friends greeted Simon with the same remark: "My, how tall you are." Yes, it was true, Simon was taller than most boys in fifth grade, but hearing it said out loud so much always made him feel bashful.

And once they'd finished commenting on his height, they'd always say, "And look at that great hair! Where'd you get those curls?" (Simon was often tempted to answer that he'd sent away for them from the back of a cereal box. But of course he never did.) Then they always added, "Why do boys get all the curls?"

Simon would stare at the ground, blushing and waiting for the freckle comment. "Well, say, did you ever see so many freckles in your life?" they'd ask, as if they were the first person to notice them. Then they'd make the freckle joke. "Bet you could play connect the dots with those freckles! Ha-ha-ha!"

The more Simon thought about Aunt Mattie, the more amazed—and grateful—he was that she hadn't made a single one of the tall/curly hair/freckle remarks. Instead, she had asked him what *he* thought of *her*.

"Well," said Simon slowly. "I thought you'd be . . ."

"Taller? Thinner?" asked Aunt Mattie. And she laughed—a little bit like geese honking in a snowstorm, he decided. Nothing at all like the genteel titter that was his mother's laugh, or the polite smile that his father often wore, or Aunt Bea's loud bray. Watching her, Simon was upset to see that she closed her eyes each time she laughed. The car wobbled onto the edge of the road and then back again. Simon closed his eyes, too.

How does she manage to read my mind like that? he wondered. Maybe she *is* a witch.

That would explain why no one in his house ever mentioned her name. And why, when his mother had had to find somewhere for Simon to stay during spring vacation, the last person she'd thought of was his great-aunt Matilda.

"Aunt Matilda?" Uncle Fred had asked in surprise. "*My* aunt Matilda?"

"Yes," Mrs. Maxwell had said. "She's George's aunt, too." George was Simon's father, who was in Japan on a business trip just then.

Uncle Fred had raised his eyebrows just a tiny bit, which meant he didn't approve. "Isn't she sort of . . . *you know?*"

"Is she?" Mrs. Maxwell had said. "I've never actually met her. But I just don't have any choice. No one else can take him while you're staying here."

So it was decided: during spring vacation, Simon would go to stay with his great-aunt in the country. That way, Aunt Bea and Uncle Fred could move into the Maxwells' only guest room. And their son, the loathsome cousin Parker, would have Simon's room. And Simon smiled and was brave about it, even though he didn't want Parker in his room. Even though he didn't want to go away. Even though he'd never met Great-aunt Matilda. And even though she was a bit *"you know."*

Simon had worried for weeks about what *"you know"* could mean. Did it mean she was nasty—a coldhearted child-hater? Or horribly strict? Or perhaps extremely old and fussy? Now that the dreadful day had come, he glanced over at his great-aunt. He could be wrong, but she didn't seem coldhearted, or cranky. Or fussy.

Was she a witch, then? Is that what *"you know"* meant?

Too Much Bother

Simon's thoughts were interrupted as the car drove into a dirt driveway and came to a halt in a hail of flying gravel outside a ramshackle red farmhouse.

A row of very tall, very bright salmon-colored flowers drooped by the front door. A swaybacked old white horse stood on the porch, calmly eating daffodils out of the window box. Two brilliant green peacocks perched on the chimney. Against the front porch leaned an old motorcycle that someone had taken apart and never put back together. And beside that was an amazingly ugly carved wooden bed. From the paddock by the barn, a trio of camels stared suspiciously at Aunt Mattie and Simon as they got out of the car.

Inside, the house was even stranger. An enormous rubber-tree plant grew up one wall and across the length of the ceiling, suspended by threads. Stacked everywhere were books and magazines and junk. There were tennis rackets with no strings, skis with no bindings, and golf clubs with no heads. Most startling were the cats—at least a dozen of them draped about here and there like cast-off clothing.

"Please, please, don't get up," said Aunt Mattie to the cats at large. She flung her hat onto a table and collapsed onto the only piece of furniture in sight, a huge lumpy sofa. "Confusticate these cats!" she exclaimed as several that she had sat on protested loudly, wriggling out from under her bulk. A small cloud of cat hair was released into the air, and Simon noticed that the couch was thick with it. Imagine the dirt, he thought. Imagine the mess. Imagine the fleas.

Aunt Mattie turned to Simon. "Now, then, young Simon. Here you are in the country. I'm sorry you can't meet Uncle Philbert until tomorrow—he's off visiting a sick relative. But your wish is my command. What would you like to do?"

Simon looked at his feet and mumbled. "I don't know—whatever you like. I don't want to be any bother."

"Bother!" snorted Mattie. "Bother is what I like best. People who are no bother are like . . . like *furniture*. Furniture is absolutely no bother at all. That's why I have so little of it. Cats, on the other hand, are nothing *but* bother. The same with plants. Always needing something: a bit of water or fertilizer, a pruning—I'm talking about the plants, not the cats—or to be let in, or to be let out, or to be fed, or petted, or brushed—the cats, that is, not the plants."

There was a long pause.

Mattie glanced at her grandfather clock, whose hands stood at nine o'clock.

"Goodness, it's . . . it's . . ." She grabbed a pencil and

wrote some figures on an old envelope. "And carry the eleven makes . . . It's quarter past twelve. Snack time. Come and talk to me while I make it. Then we'll go out and meet the animals."

Simon followed his great-aunt silently into the kitchen, where a pair of cats were sleeping in the warming oven of a vast iron cookstove. The stove gave off a delicious warmth. A smell of fresh baking filled the air.

"You look confused, Simon," said Mattie. "Don't you want a snack?"

"In our house," Simon said in a voice that was hardly louder than a whisper, "snack time is at ten-thirty, and twelve o'clock is lunchtime."

"Shut your mutt!"

Instead, Simon let his mouth sag wide open.

"What?" he asked in a whisper.

"Say please!" came the peevish order again. But this time, Simon could see that it didn't come from his aunt, but from a gray parrot that was clinging upside down to an overhead lamp.

"Oh, really, Runcible." Mattie sighed. "You are a contumelious creature. Is that any way to greet my long-lost nephew?" The parrot stopped combing her feathers with her beak and looked at Mattie.

"Stuff it," said the bird, adding for good measure, "dog breath."

Mattie shook her head. "She's quite incorrigible," she said as she put a kettle onto the cookstove to boil. "It's best to ignore her."

"Now, about the question of snack time: in this house, it's snack time whenever we decide to have a snack. Let's see what we have here."

She went over to a row of crockery jars on the counter and began opening them. The one marked FLOUR contained bright red pistachio nuts. The one marked SUGAR contained black licorice sticks. The one marked COFFEE contained a heap of chunky cookies. Mattie sniffed them.

"Butterscotch-peppermint cookies," she said, "I

think. Or perhaps they're chocolate-raspberry. Might have to try one to be sure." She took a large bite. "Butterscotch-raspberry without a doubt," she said, with her mouth full of cookie. "What would you like?"

"I don't mind," said Simon. So Mattie filled a plate with pistachio nuts and butterscotch-raspberry cookies and went to the cupboard.

"Now for tea," she said.

Simon, trying hard to be polite, said, "I'm not allowed to drink tea."

"I'm glad to hear it," said Mattie. "Why would anyone want to? It's a filthy drink made from ground-up leaves, for goodness sake. I don't drink it, either. Same with coffee—dried beans soaked in warm water! Yuck! *And* it turns your teeth brown." She shuddered. "Sometimes it amazes me what otherwise-normal human beings will eat or drink."

Simon smiled, and Mattie kept going.

"Consider wine," she said as she put out mugs and took the kettle off the stove. "Wine is made from rotten grapes. Rotten grapes! Did you ever taste it?"

"Once," said Simon, making a face.

"Exactly," said Mattie. "Now then, for tea I'm afraid we don't have any of the ground-up leaves, but we do have"—she read the labels of some jars—"ginger tea, raspberry tea, cinnamon tea, or peach tea."

Simon started to say, "I don't mind" again, then stopped. "Ginger sounds interesting," he said.

"That's the spirit. How do you take your tea? Milk? Sugar? Ice cream?"

"Just plain, please," Simon murmured.

She poured them both out steaming mugs, adding a

dollop of vanilla ice cream to hers. Simon simply gaped, until he remembered that it was not polite to stare.

"Say thank you!"

"Thank you," said Simon automatically. Then he realized it had been Runcible, the parrot, speaking, not Aunt Mattie, and he blushed.

"Now then," said Aunt Mattie, taking a gulp of ginger tea. "Tell me, how are your parents?"

"They're fine," said Simon rapidly, thinking of his father, who was never home, and when he was home never had time for anything but sleeping. He began to apologize for his parents. "Mother and Father wish they could have driven me, but Father's boss called at the last minute and said he had to go on a business trip. And Mother had to stay to help Aunt Bea unpack her things and—"

But Aunt Mattie simply laughed at this apology, as if it were the most natural thing in the world for parents to have put their young son on a train to visit a great-aunt he'd never met.

"Your father came to stay with me once. But I haven't seen him since he was ten years old. How old are you now, Simon?"

"I'll be eleven in two weeks, after vacation." Simon knew that it was polite for Mattie to ask him how old *he* was. But it would be rude for him to ask her how old *she* was—yet another grown-up rule he didn't understand. So he kept quiet. To his surprise, she volunteered the information.

"I'm seventy-two," she said. "And a half."

"That's nice," said Simon, thinking it was incredibly old.

"Now tell me about yourself, Simon. How do you like school? I assume you go to some sort of school?"

"It's very nice, thank you," said the boy, looking into his mug and thinking of the long gray building he went to every day.

"And your teacher, do you like her?"

"Yes," said Simon without looking up. He was thinking of Mrs. Biggs. Mrs. Biggs was rude to all the boys—and even some of the girls—in his class. All but him. She was never rude to Simon because Simon was always quiet and well behaved. He never talked without raising his hand first. He always knew the right answer. Mrs. Biggs loved Simon.

"And do you have lots of friends?"

"Oh yes," said Simon quickly. "Lots and lots."

"I see," said Aunt Mattie softly. Then she added, "Simon, you're not drinking your tea. Don't you like it?"

"Oh yes," Simon said. "It's very nice, thank you." He took a little sip. It was scalding and burned his lip. He gasped.

"Dear me, it's too hot," said Aunt Mattie. "That's why I always put ice cream in. I'm sorry. Did you hurt yourself?"

"Not at all," said Simon, blinking back tears of pain. "It's just right." And to prove it to her, he took another sip, and burned his lip again. "Just fine, thank you."

Aunt Mattie gave him a long look.

"You Maxwell boys," she said to herself, "you're all the same. I can see I have lots of work to do." And to Simon's deep and lasting astonishment, she leaned back in her seat, put her handkerchief to her mouth, and burped loudly.

After Aunt Mattie burped—or "belched," as his mother would have called it—Simon was so shocked that he hardly noticed what happened next.

Aunt Mattie jabbed her thumb into her forehead, looked at Simon, and then reached over and punched him lightly on the shoulder.

"There," she said happily. "That's what we do in this house when someone burps."

"What?" asked Simon. "You what?"

"If someone burps," said Mattie cheerily, "everyone has to stick their thumb to their forehead. The last person in the room to do it gets punched." Simon started to smile and Mattie looked very pleased. "What do you do in *your* house?"

"In our house," said Simon, and he stopped smiling, "if you burp—I mean, belch—you get sent to your room."

"Goodness!" exclaimed Mattie. "Even your parents? How interesting."

"Of course not," said Simon. "My parents never get sent to their room."

"Even when they burp? That's not fair."

"My parents never belch," explained Simon.

"They don't?"

"No. It's very rude, you know. Oh, I'm sorry, I didn't mean that you—"

"Not at all," said Mattie happily. "What you say is most interesting. Who says it's rude to burp?"

"Well, my parents, and, well—everyone does."

"Everyone? Did you know that in many countries it is considered *polite* to belch after a meal?"

"No!" Simon was shocked.

"Yes, in Germany, for example, it is a sign that you enjoyed your meal. It is a compliment to the cook. And, Simon?"

"Yes?"

"In this house, it is considered polite to burp. Okay?"

Simon smiled. "Okay," he said.

Mattie laughed. Goose honks on a snowy day, thought Simon. Definitely.

So Many Questions

"Come along Simon. I'll introduce you to the llamas. You'll like them. They're extremely nasty."

Simon trotted obediently behind Aunt Mattie. He was full of questions, simply bursting. He couldn't help wishing that it wasn't bad manners to pepper someone with questions, the way Aunt Mattie had peppered him. He wanted to know why Aunt Mattie always liked to be fifteen minutes late, where she sat when the sofa was full, how the peacocks got on the roof, why her tennis rackets had no strings, whether she really was a witch.

But he kept his mouth shut, as he had been taught.

"Why so silent, Simon?"

"Well, Mother says never to speak until spoken to. And Father says it's rude to ask too many questions."

Mattie turned, her hands on her wide hips. She opened her mouth to say something, then closed it again. After a bit, she said simply, "Your father appears to have forgotten everything I ever taught him. I think it's rude *not* to ask questions. Seems like you're not interested."

"Oh, but—"

"Take my sofa, for instance—never asks any questions at all, and I think that's because it finds me boring. Am I boring you, Simon?"

Simon smiled, and ran to keep up with her. He couldn't remember when he had felt *less* bored. "No, Aunt Mattie."

"The *sofa*," continued Aunt Mattie, striding off as if she hadn't heard him, "the sofa never speaks until spoken to. Have you ever stopped to think, young Simon, what the world would be like if *no one* ever spoke until spoken to? Hmm?"

"Well—"

"It would be an awfully quiet place, Simon. And it would make using the phone difficult, now wouldn't it?"

Simon tried to imagine a phone conversation in which no one was allowed to talk first. He smiled. Then Mattie started giggling—there was no other word for it—and Simon felt himself starting to laugh. It was a small laugh, but it grew and grew until his sides ached, and he had to wrap his arms around his ribs and sit down. Aunt Mattie, meanwhile, was gasping for breath, and pretty soon she had to sit down, too.

After they had caught their breath, Mattie looked at Simon, but he remained silent. At last she said, "What else do your parents say?"

"What?"

" 'Don't speak till spoken to.' 'Don't ask questions.' I'll bet they also say, 'Children should be seen and not heard.' Am I right?"

Simon shook his head. She *was* a witch! "How did you know?"

"And probably: 'Don't speak with your mouth full' and 'Don't eat with your mouth open.' Or is it: 'Don't eat with your mouth full' and 'Don't speak with your mouth open'?"

Simon smiled at the thought of trying to speak without opening his mouth. Or eating only when his mouth was empty.

"And then at mealtime they tell you to sit down, and once you sit down, they tell you to sit *up*. Which is it—up or down?"

"You seem to know a lot about our house," said Simon.

"Well," said Mattie solemnly, "I know a lot about Maxwells. And I know a lot about grown-ups." She struggled to her feet. "Let's go find those llamas. They don't have any silly rules. In fact, they are the rudest creatures on God's earth."

What Simon had taken for camels were in fact long-haired brown-and-white llamas. They were named Mr. Rude, Mr. Crude, and Mr. Ugly. All three crowded over to inspect him when Mattie was filling their feed troughs. As Simon watched, the biggest llama, Mr. Ugly, curled back his lips and spat at him. A big gob of llama spittle struck Simon in the middle of his neat button-down white shirt. Simon yelped.

"Disgusting dromedaries!" shouted Mattie, shaking her fist at them. "Flocculent, flea-bitten varmints! Why," she said to Simon, "they'd as soon spit at you as look at you. They're utterly good-for-nothing."

Simon, starting to smile, looked down at the brown stain on his shirt and thought of what his mother would say about it. His smile vanished.

Aunt Mattie seemed, as usual, to be reading his thoughts.

"Back at the house," she said, "I have a bottle of Sure-fire Llama Spit Stain Remover. Your poor shirt! It's entirely my fault, dearie. I should never have brought you out here in your best Sunday going-to-meeting clothes. Let's go in and change."

"Into what?"

"Why, into some work clothes."

"But I don't have any."

Mattie surveyed his spotless gray school pants, his shiny leather shoes, his neatly pressed shirt, his blue blazer (he'd taken the tie off in the train and stuffed it in his pocket).

"What's in that suitcase, then? No blue jeans?"

"No."

"No T-shirts?"

"No."

"No sneakers?"

"No. My mother packed for me, and she insisted that I bring lots of nice clothes. All I've got is school clothes like this."

"Well." Her hands perched on her hips in disbelief. "We'll have to do something about that. But for now, I'll take you to meet the horses."

First was the old white nag that had been on the porch.

"That's Sugar," said Mattie. "And she's even older than I am. In horse years, of course. Imagine that." Sugar put out her head for the sugar cube that Mattie had brought in her pocket. Simon, who'd always been told that horses bite, touched her muzzle cautiously. He was trying to work up his courage to ask about riding her when another horse cantered up. This was a shaggy young chestnut, and he shook his head and danced nervously around Mattie while she held out a carrot for him. Simon thought him the most beautiful horse he'd ever seen.

"His name is Hero, and he's a love," said Mattie. "He's mad about carrots."

"Can I ride him?" asked Simon, forgetting his manners

in his excitement. He added hastily, "That is, if it's not too much trouble for you."

"I'm sorry, dear," said his aunt. "You can't ride him. No one can. You see, the man who owned him before me was a beast. He was vicious to Hero. One day, Hero decided he'd had enough, and he bucked that man off. Nearly killed him. And from that day on, Hero wouldn't let anyone on his back. He was on his way to the glue factory when I bought him. And the longer it's been since a horse has been ridden, the wilder he is."

"Why did you buy a horse that no one can ride?"

"Because I admired him so much. He stood up for himself, even though it almost cost him his life. That's why I named him Hero."

"What about Sugar?"

"She's too old to be ridden. I got her at the glue factory, too. You see, I'm too old to be ridden, too. Oh, you know what I mean—too old to be any use to anyone. And I kept wondering what it would be like if someone sent *me* to the glue factory."

"Why do you have llamas if they're 'good-for-nothing'?"

"Because they don't take any guff from anyone."

"What do you mean?"

"They won't let anyone else push them around. I like that in an animal. You notice I don't have any 'useful' animals like sheep or cows or chickens. They're such goody-goodies. Just sit there doing what they're told. They make wool. They give milk. They lay eggs. So dull! I like animals who are rude and don't cooperate—animals that are lots of bother and no earthly use to anyone. Like cats. Or peacocks. They spend all day looking at themselves in the mirror. Why, just try asking *peacocks* to lay eggs or do something useful!"

"Or the parrot," said Simon. "She'd probably insult you!"

"Absolutely," said Mattie. "That's why I'm so fond of her. She's like Hero, no use to anyone. The pet-store owner couldn't sell her, because of her foul mouth. And he couldn't keep her in the store anymore because she was driving away customers. One day, a woman came in and asked what she could do about her macaw—that's a large bird—who was feeling poorly. And just as the owner opened his mouth, Runcible said, 'Stuff it!' Just like that."

Mattie emitted some loud honks of laughter. "The lady turned on her heel and stormed out of the pet store. And Runcible yelled after her, 'Put a sock in it!' Why, the poor store owner practically *paid* me to take Runcible away."

Simon laughed, remembering the shock he'd felt when Runcible first insulted him in the kitchen. "And why do you always—"

Mattie raised her eyebrows. "My goodness, but you're suddenly full of questions."

"I—I'm sorry," stammered Simon. "It's just—you said you liked ques—"

"The more the better. Carry on. You may speak without being spoken to."

"Well, I was going to ask you why you always try to be fifteen minutes late. I thought it was rude to be late." Then he blushed, thinking that what he had just said sounded extremely rude.

To his surprise Mattie laughed. "Yes, terribly," she

agreed. "But so much more exciting that way, don't you think? What did you do while you were waiting at the station for me?"

"Well, I watched a spider catching a fly. She wrapped it up as tight as she could in her—"

"You see!" interrupted Aunt Mattie. That was another thing about Aunt Mattie. She interrupted all the time. She seemed not to know that was bad manners. "Now, if I'd arrived on time," she said, "you would have missed the spider and the fly! Thank heavens I remembered to forget."

"Forget what?" asked Simon.

"The time your train arrived, silly. Anything else you want to know?"

"Yes," said Simon. "Why is your furniture outdoors, in the yard? Won't that bed get ruined?"

"Oh, yes. I hope so. It's like leftovers."

"Leftovers?"

"Yes. You know, when you have a little of something left over from a meal, not enough to eat, but you can't quite bear to throw it out. So you put it in a container at the back of the fridge for a month or so until it goes all green and moldy. Then you open it up and say, 'Yuck!' And *then* you can throw it out."

"You *want* to throw out your furniture?"

"Oh yes. I've told you: furniture is boring. That bed was given to me by *my* great-aunt. It's some sort of antique, you see, a family heirloom. So I couldn't just take it to the dump. And nobody in their right mind would actually buy it, it's so ugly. So I'm euthanizing it first."

"What's that?"

"It means to put something out of its misery—like

when you have a very old, sick pet put to sleep. I had to do that to a plant once, too."

"You put a plant out of its misery?"

"Yes. A cactus. Someone gave it to me—why I can't imagine. Oh, it was the most boring, miserable plant in the world. Never grew, never blossomed. Never did anything. Just sat there looking like a pincushion. Of course I overwatered it. I kept thinking if I gave it some more water, something might actually happen. Well, to make a long story short, one winter night I put it out on the porch and put it out of its misery. It was a quick and painless death.

"Now, what else would you like to know? Don't be shy."

"Well . . . why do you have tennis rackets without any strings?"

"Because they're for people who are only a little bit interested in playing tennis," replied Aunt Mattie, looking stern. "You know the kind: they come to visit and you say, 'Would you like to play tennis?' and they say, 'Well, sure, I guess,' and so you get out the rackets and they look at them and say, 'Oh gosh, that's too bad,' and it saves them the trouble of having to do something they really don't like. The same with those golf clubs."

"I see," said Simon, who didn't.

Sometimes talking to Aunt Mattie made him feel dizzy.

That night, as Aunt Mattie was tucking him in, she said, "Uncle Philbert will be home later tonight. He's a terrible curmudgeon, but I'm going to ask him to give you lessons."

Simon's heart sank. He didn't know what a curmudgeon was, but it didn't sound great. "That's very kind of you, Aunt Mattie," he said. "But really, I'm taking piano and French lessons already at—"

"Not French lessons, silly," said his aunt.

"Then what are they?"

"Let's just say they're called . . . well, un-lessons."

"What are—"

"Tomorrow," said his aunt. "You'll see."

How Do You Do?

Next morning, Simon lay in bed, not quite awake, and thought, as one does, that he was at home. Any moment he would be awakened by his mother's knock and her cheerful morning greeting: "Rise and shine." She would come into his room with an armful of freshly ironed shirts and pants for school, pull the curtains, and give him a peck on the cheek.

Instead, what happened was, Simon started to choke. This may have had something to do with Raspberry, a large, warm, ginger-colored cat who had climbed onto his pillow, settled comfortably on Simon's head, and placed his tail in Simon's mouth. When Simon objected to this, dislodging Raspberry as gently as possible, the cat shot him a look as if to say, *Really! How rude!* Then he settled onto Simon's chest, put his nose up against Simon's nose, and purred loudly.

Simon lay there, stroking Raspberry and wondering what it was about waking up in a strange bed that could make you feel so suddenly homesick. Probably just that everything seemed so different. Not bad. Just different.

He thought back to last night's amazing dinner. It had started off with a large slice of lemon meringue pie. "No vegetables or chicken for you, young man, until you've finished your pie," Aunt Mattie had said sternly as she set it before him. Needless to say, he ate the whole piece. And then when she produced the chicken and peas and potatoes, she hadn't minded a bit when he hadn't finished his peas.

As Simon lay there, delicious smells began wafting up from the kitchen. The last thing his mother had said to him was, "Don't wake Aunt Matilda and Uncle Philbert up in the mornings. Old people like to sleep late. Wait till she wakes you."

But she might never come to wake him. And the smells coming from the kitchen proved she was already awake. So Simon finally decided to go downstairs. Just as he walked into the kitchen, his great-aunt opened one of the many doors in the cookstove and removed a large pizza. It was bubbling hot. She dislodged a cat from one of the warming ovens and replaced it with the pizza.

"Homemade," said Mattie proudly. "Sit right down and I'll cut you a slice. Now then, how does your corporosity seem to gashiate today?"

Once again, Simon was speechless. "Pizza for breakfast?" he asked finally.

"And fruit salad," said his aunt, serving him a generous triangle of gooey pizza, along with a bowl of sliced oranges, pineapples, and bananas. "Something wrong?"

"Oh, no, no, not at all. It's just . . . well . . . I don't usually . . ."

"Have pizza for breakfast?"

"No."

"Why on earth not?"

"I guess it's not good for you."

"What *do* you usually have for breakfast?"

"Oh, I have the same thing every morning: Super Frosted Rice Poppies with marshmallows."

"And *that's* good for you?"

"Well, it is kinda sugary—"

"Do you ever have pizza for dinner or lunch?"

"Yes."

"And *then* it's good for you? But in the morning it's not?"

"Well, I—"

"It is just a question of what you are used to, isn't it? Did you know that in England they have smoked fish for breakfast, and sometimes kidneys?"

"Disgusting!"

"And other countries have goat cheese for breakfast."

"Gross!"

"The Japanese have rice for breakfast."

"Yuck!"

" 'Yuck'? What do you think Rice Poppies are made of?"

"I . . . well, rice, I guess, but—"

"And another thing. What would you say to your mother if she gave you the same thing for lunch every single day of your life?"

"I would get really bored of it and ask for something else."

"But you can eat the same thing every morning for breakfast—cereal and orange juice—and never get bored?"

"Gee, I never thought of it like that."

"Maybe you should try it, hmm?"

Simon looked at his pizza. Suddenly, it looked very tasty.

He was spared from having to answer Aunt Mattie by the banging of the screen door. A man in faded overalls and a plaid shirt entered the kitchen, pulled out a chair, and sat down.

"You're late," said Mattie.

"Good," said the man gruffly. "I do my best." He had longish silvery hair, a droopy white mustache, and appeared about the same age as Mattie. Unlike Mattie, however, he was long and lean as a garden rake. He turned to Simon for the first time, and Simon felt a little scared. Uncle Philbert—he assumed this man must be Uncle Philbert—reminded him of the extremely grouchy grandfather in the book *Heidi*. Simon had an uncomfortable feeling that he was about to find out just exactly what the word *curmudgeon* meant. He took a deep breath and addressed his great-uncle as he had been taught to do.

"How do you do?" said Simon politely.

"What?" asked the man.

"I said, 'How do you do?' " repeated Simon loudly.

"No need to shout," said the man. "I'm not deaf. I heard you very well the first time. And I answered you: 'What?' "

"Excuse me?" asked Simon.

"How do I do *what*?" said the man grumpily. "How do I do crossword puzzles? How do I do my laundry? How do I do long division? Different answer for each question, isn't there?"

Simon had once read a book about a girl named Alice who went down a rabbit hole and met a large caterpillar that was very rude to her. Right now, he felt a lot like Alice.

"You'll be Simon," the man said between mouthfuls of pizza.

Suddenly, instead of feeling scared, Simon felt mad.

"I'll be Simon," he said slowly, "if you'll be Uncle Philbert."

To Simon's surprise, Philbert—for it was he—laughed so hard at this that awful things happened to the tablecloth. After Mattie had sponged up the table and wiped the tears from her own eyes, she turned to Uncle Philbert.

"That's one for Simon," she said happily.

"Humph!" snorted Philbert. "I thought you told me the kid was too polite for his own good."

"Well, he's a fast learner. All it took was ten minutes of being around the rudest man in the world. Now I will leave you two together while I feed the animals. You can get started right in on your un-lessons."

When Aunt Mattie got back from feeding the animals, Simon and Uncle Philbert were still sitting at the kitchen table. Uncle Philbert had his hand under his shirt, cupped under his armpit. He looked a little embarrassed when Mattie walked in.

"I was just starting him off with an un-lesson on Rude Noises," he explained. Then he added gruffly, "Can you believe this boy is nearly eleven years old and no one has ever taught him how to make armpit noises? What kind of an education you gettin' in them schools anyhow?

That's right, you just kind of put your hand there and squeeze. Good, excellent."

Simon giggled. He had just made a noise that sounded remarkably like Uncle Fred blowing his nose.

"Uncle Philbert, why are they called un-lessons?"

"Why, some of it's stuff you got to un-learn, you see? And others is just stuff that you can't be a real kid unless'n you know how to do it. Now then, my boy, can you spit?"

Simon shook his head.

"Well, I'll be pickled. I really will. You poor neglected child. Come on outside and I'll show you."

Un-lessons

The next four or five days went by in a blur for Simon.

He got used to waking up with the cat Raspberry in his mouth. In fact, it soon got so he couldn't sleep without Raspberry purring gently on his head.

He got used to having strange food: pizza, macaroni, baked apples for breakfast; cake or pie for dinner, with vegetables for dessert. In fact, after several days of eating pie for dinner, he discovered that he sort of looked forward to the peas and carrots.

He got used to ginger tea served at all times of the day. In fact, he found it was totally delicious, especially with ice cream to cool it down.

He even learned the answer to the ritual morning question about how his "corporosity seemed to gashiate." The answer, apparently, was, "Very discombobulate, great congruity, dissimilarity." When Simon asked Philbert what this nonsense meant, Philbert answered, "Who knows? All I know is, it makes about as much sense as being asked how you 'do' and answering, 'Fine.' Tell me what *that* means!"

Uncle Philbert and Aunt Mattie seemed determined to fill in the gaps in Simon's appalling education. Each morning started with an un-lesson after breakfast. Within a day, Simon was making great armpit noises. He could even manage to "play tunes" like "Yankee Doodle."

Spitting, however, was harder, and Simon was practicing on the front porch the second morning when Philbert asked him if he'd brought his jackknife with him. "I want to teach you how to whittle," he explained.

"I don't have a knife," said Simon. Then, seeing Philbert's look of disbelief, he added, "My parents are afraid I might cut myself."

Uncle Philbert just nodded a few times. "You can borrow mine," he said at last. Simon reached for the beautiful bone-handled knife, enjoying the heft of it in his palm, and Philbert showed him how to unfold the blades safely. He handed him a stick of poplar. "Got to start with a soft wood. Now, always whittle away from yourself," he said, demonstrating with a few quick flicks that removed the bark. Simon whittled slowly and carefully, and pretty soon the poplar stick was smoothed out on all sides, shiny and white.

"What are we going to make with it?" asked Simon.

"Make?" said Philbert, looking shocked again. "You don't 'make' anything. You just whittle for the fun of whittlin'. To get it nice and smooth. Can't we do something purely for the heck of it?"

"Well, some people"—namely his father—"might say that was a waste of time," said Simon.

"That's exactly right," said Uncle Philbert. "It's a grand way to waste some time."

They both smiled and took turns whittling for a while. Then Philbert took the jackknife and showed Simon how to play a game called "mumblety-peg." You used the rounded hole-puncher blade and took turns with the knife, balancing the tip first on your finger, then on your

knee, then on your foot and all different parts of your body. The point was to toss it up in the air in such a way that the blade stuck straight into the ground when it landed. Each time it stuck in, you got another turn. As Simon managed an expert toss with his foot, he wondered what his mother would think if she could see him now.

Another day, Philbert showed Simon how to make an earsplitting whistle with two fingers in his mouth. For Simon, who had only just discovered how to whistle in the usual way, this was much harder to learn. He practiced everywhere he went for two days, making a circle with thumb and forefinger, placing them over his folded-back tongue, and blowing hard. Sometimes he nearly fainted from dizziness as he blew over and over. But nothing came out, not even a squeak. Then, suddenly, on the third day, an extraordinary sound came from his mouth. It was so loud, it startled him. He blew again. Another sharp whistle. It was the most piercing noise he had ever heard.

As he practiced, an even more surprising thing happened. Hero, who had been far out in the pasture, heard him and came trotting up to the fence. Simon laughed and reached timidly out to touch his head. "Now we have a secret signal, old pal," he said. And Hero shook his mane, as if agreeing.

A Warning

Finally, the day came when they could no longer put off buying Simon some work clothes.

Philbert said he'd rather die and go to purgatory than go clothes shopping, so he went outside to mow the lawn. But when Mattie and Simon went out to get in the car, they found Uncle Philbert glaring at the lawn mower. He had yanked on the handle to start the mower, and the handle had come right off in his hand.

"Confusticate this machine!" he shouted. "You misbegotten metal monster!" He aimed a kick at a rear wheel, which promptly fell off. "You, you son-of-a-tractor!"

Aunt Mattie gave him a knowing look and fetched him a pair of handheld shears. "Why don't you try these, dear? Even you can't break these."

But Uncle Philbert insisted on going into town with them to buy a new part for the lawn mower, so they all piled into the old car.

This time, Simon sat in back so Philbert could have the

passenger seat. The goldfish were still there, and Simon was instructed to "do something to cheer them up." The backseat, which was apparently seldom used to transport human beings, was heaped with library books, garden tools, jigsaw puzzles, blankets, and magazines with titles like *The Compleat Guide to Llama Care*. Mattie threw the car into reverse, and they lurched out of the driveway and onto the road. Once again, Simon found himself gripping the door handle to keep from falling off the seat. It was all he could do to hold the goldfish bowl upright.

"Awfully quiet in the backseat," sang out Aunt Mattie after several minutes. "Are we boring you?"

"No, Aunt Mattie," said Simon.

"Good. Then, let's play fifty questions."

"How do you play that?"

"Well, you ask fifty questions, and I answer them."

Simon laughed. "Okay. Why is it that you do all the driving? In most of the families I know, the father always drives."

"That's because—" Philbert started to say, but as usual, he was interrupted.

"I'm a much better driver than Philbert." Mattie laughed.

"Mendacious woman!" sputtered Philbert. He turned around to look at Simon. "The real reason is, Mattie has a magic way with machines. You take this car, for instance. It's a 1946 New York taxicab. It had two hundred thousand miles on it. Like just about everything else we own, it was on its way to the glue factory, or whatever it's called—"

"The scrap pile," suggested Mattie.

"But she bought it for fifty dollars. Then she got a few books on engine repair, took the whole thing apart, right there in our front yard. Put it all back together again, and this car has purred like a pastry for the last ten years."

"Philbert," said Mattie, pursing her lips, "pastry doesn't purr."

"Did Uncle Philbert help you repair the car?"

"Uncle Philbert!" said Mattie with an explosive laugh. "Why, if Bertie even gets within spitting distance of an engine—any kind of engine—it keels straight over and dies. They wilt like salted snails. The man has a curse on him."

"Sad but true," admitted Uncle Philbert, looking at the lawn mower handle.

"On the other hand," said Mattie, "he is wonderful with the animals. Even the llamas behave for him."

Gradually during this conversation, Simon had become aware of something strange going on behind him. He turned to peer out the back window. And gasped. A police car was following right behind them. And its blue lights were flashing. Simon knew what that meant: Trouble with a capital *T*. He looked at Mattie. She appeared not to have noticed anything amiss.

"Aunt Mattie," said Simon in a croaky voice, "there's a police car behind us."

"Yes, dear," said Mattie, and kept right on driving and chatting with Philbert.

Simon didn't know what to do next. His father had once gotten a speeding ticket, and Simon had hidden under the backseat during the whole awful thing. His father had grown red in the face and said terrible things under his breath as he pulled off the road. Then the policeman had sauntered over to their car, knocked on the driver's window, and demanded to see his father's license and registration. Simon, lying on the floor, felt overcome with shame and embarrassment. He had never been sent to the principal's office and made to sit in the red chair in the hall so that everyone walking by would know he had been bad. But this must be exactly what it felt like. He wondered if his father was feeling that way. As the officer gave him a one-hundred-dollar speeding ticket, Mr. Maxwell had been terribly polite. "Yes, Officer." And "No,

Officer." And "I'm sorry, Officer. It won't happen again." Simon hadn't known which was worse, the sight of his father getting caught breaking the law or the awful, polite way he'd talked to the policeman.

Simon looked at Mattie nervously. Why didn't she pull off the road? But his great-aunt continued driving merrily down the road, seemingly unconcerned about the lights flashing inches behind her car. Simon peeked out the back. He could see the policeman's face growing stern and red. Suddenly, the patrol car pulled out beside Aunt Mattie. The policeman gestured with his arm to her to pull over. Mattie gave him an icy look.

At last, the police car swerved in front of them, forcing Aunt Mattie off the road, onto the dirt shoulder. She stopped the car, and the police cruiser pulled up a few feet in front of them.

Now she's really gonna get it, thought Simon. Reckless driving, refusing to stop for a police officer, speeding, resisting arrest. He was sure they put you in prison for that. Maybe they'd arrest her on the spot. He glanced at his aunt with deep concern. But she looked neither worried nor angry. She looked stern.

Suddenly, Mattie turned off the engine. Before the policeman could budge from his car, Mattie hopped out and strode briskly over to his door. She rapped smartly on his window with her car keys. The policeman, who was talking on his car radio, looked at her in astonishment. He hung up his radio receiver and rolled down the window.

"Young man," said Mattie, "what on earth do you mean by driving like that?"

"What?" said the officer, a look of disbelief on his face.

"You heard me," snapped Mattie. "You were tailgating

me—a very dangerous practice to drive so close to another car. And then you passed me in a 'no passing' zone. Are you aware that you passed me on a solid yellow line?"

"What?" said the officer again.

"And all that gesturing and swerving in front of me like that! Why, we could have had a terrible accident!" Mattie paused and peered inside the patrol car. "Young man, are you aware that your seat belt is not fastened? Well"—she straightened up—"I'm afraid I'm going to have to take your name and badge number and report you to the police."

"What?" said the policeman again. He was beginning to sound like a broken record. "But, lady, I *am* the police." He looked around, as if hoping another patrol car might be coming to his rescue.

"You heard me," said Mattie briskly, taking a pad and pencil from her purse. She licked the end of the pencil. "Name and badge number, please."

"Now listen here, lady—" said the officer.

"And after that I'll need to see your driver's license and car registration. I urge you to cooperate. Otherwise, I might have to make a citizen's arrest."

From his seat in the car, Simon watched in amazement as the police officer climbed out of his cruiser. He handed his badge, license, and registration over to Mattie. Next he closed his eyes and touched his finger to his nose. Then Mattie had him walk a straight line along the edge of the road.

"What's she doing?" Simon asked Philbert.

"Sobriety test," answered Philbert, as if he'd seen this sort of thing before.

"What's that?"

"It's a test the police give you—touch your nose, walk a straight line—to make sure you haven't been drinkin' alcohol. Not supposed to drink and drive, you see."

"But why's *she* doing it to *him*?"

"Well, you gotta admit he was drivin' pretty strangely. Tailgatin' and flashin' his lights, and cuttin' in front of us."

"But that's what the police *always* do when you're supposed to pull over."

"Really?" said Philbert, sounding interested. "Darn stupid way to carry on, if you ask me."

Just then, Mattie returned to the car. She squeezed herself into the seat, started the engine, and pulled the car back onto the road. They passed the police officer. He was sitting in his cruiser, resting his head limply on the steering wheel.

"Just fancy," said Mattie, as they lurched along. "*He* was going to give *me* a ticket!"

"What happened?" asked Simon, still unable to believe Mattie hadn't been hauled away in handcuffs.

"Oh, he was such a sweet young man," said Mattie. "I let him off with a warning."

Have a Good One

At length, they arrived at the store. It was in a mall that stretched off into the distance. Aunt Mattie drove around, looking for a parking space amid the sea of cars that glittered in the sun. Finally, they found a woman who was leaving, and Aunt Mattie waited patiently for her to pull out.

"Hate the mall," grumped Uncle Philbert in the front seat. "Why couldn't we go to the five-and-dime on Main Street?"

"I would have, dear, but they closed when the mall opened." Aunt Mattie turned to Simon in the back. "Why, three years ago, this used to be apple orchards and ponds. The town had one store, the five-and-dime. It had everything you needed, and you could be done in about four minutes."

"Now we have a hundred and fifty stores to shop at," groaned Philbert. "I can never find what I need, and it takes two hours."

46

Just as the woman pulled out of Mattie's parking space, a little red MG coming from the other direction cut in front of Mattie and zoomed into the spot they had been waiting for. A man jumped out of the sports car, refused to look at them, and strode off to the stores.

Simon's father would have been furious if that had happened to him. Mattie just smiled.

"Everyone's in such a terrible hurry these days," she said. "Never a wonderful hurry or a delicious hurry. Always a terrible hurry. It's the reason most people forget their manners. Not to worry. There's room for both of us." And she pulled the heavy car up behind the snappy little MG until their bumpers were touching. Mattie's car stuck far out into the lane, but she didn't seem to mind. "Off we go," she said cheerfully.

"But Aunt Mattie," said Simon, looking back at the red sports car, wedged between Mattie's car and the car in front of it. "That man's stuck in that space until we come back."

"Is he?" asked his aunt innocently. "Why, yes, I do believe he is. As I said, people are in much too much of a hurry these days. It's bad for the heart."

As they walked past the red car, Uncle Philbert gave it a little pat on the hood. Just a friendly little pat, or so it seemed to Simon at the time.

They entered the cavelike mall, going from bright sunshine to the artificial glow of indoor lighting. Mattie seemed to know where she was going. She directed Philbert to a hardware store, then quickly found a clothing store for Simon. In a matter of a few minutes, they picked out two T-shirts, a pair of jeans, and some sneakers that suited Simon just fine.

Then they went to wait for Philbert by a little pond in the center of the mall. Simon sat beneath some fake trees that seemed to grow well in the fake sunlight, and watched the fake ducks floating in the water. At last, Philbert showed up, looking extremely cross. "It was bad enough getting lost," he fumed. "But what I really can't stand is all those people telling me to have a nice day. Maybe I want to have a *bad* day! And the sales clerk hands me the lawn mower handle in a little bag and says, 'Have a good one.'

" 'Have a good *what*?' I say.

" 'Huh?' says the clerk.

" 'Have a good nap?' I say. 'A good trip? A good *what* exactly do you want me to have?'

" 'Oh, you know,' says the clerk. 'I meant, like, enjoy.'

"Now, I ask you," sputtered Uncle Philbert, "does she really think I'm gonna *enjoy* a lawn mower handle?"

Mattie laughed and led Simon and the still-sputtering Uncle Philbert back to the car, where a small drama awaited them. The owner of the MG was pacing beside his car.

"I've been waiting for twenty minutes," he shouted when he saw them. "What do you mean by parking behind me? People like you shouldn't be allowed on the road. Now move your car—I'm in a hurry."

He jumped into his car, and Mattie peered in his window.

"Very boring," she said pleasantly, "always to be in a terrible hurry. Myself, I always try to be a little late. Makes it more fun. You should try it someday."

The man ignored this advice and attempted to start his car instead. But the only noise that came from his engine was a series of strange clicks. He groaned and tried again. Nothing happened. The man jumped out and opened the hood. Simon saw Mattie and Philbert exchange a look.

Simon's aunt walked back to her car, but rather than getting inside, she took a screwdriver out of the trunk and returned to the sports car.

"Keep out of my way, you old cow," said the man as he peered under the hood.

"I think you'll find it's the solenoid," said Mattie mildly. "A loose wire, no doubt."

"Oh, right," said the man with a sneer. Ignoring Mattie, he climbed behind the wheel and tried to start the car again. Mattie took the screwdriver, leaned under the hood, and fiddled with something. The engine sprang to life.

"What the—" exclaimed the driver.

"The solenoid," said Mattie. "It's a common problem with the 1967 MG."

And she got back into her car and drove home.

Super Hero

In his afternoons, Simon hung out at the barn.

He watched the llamas, the llamas watched him, and they had spitting contests. During un-lessons, Uncle Philbert had tried to teach Simon the Fine Art of Spitting, but Simon had never quite gotten the knack of it. The llamas won the spitting contests easily. They could spit farther and seldom missed their target. Simon's attempts to retaliate generally ended up with spittle dribbling off his chin. He could practically see the llamas laughing at him. Shirt after shirt was subjected to Matilda's bottle of Surefire Llama Spit Stain Remover. But Simon didn't give up.

One day he was sitting on the fence rail, watching the llamas eat. Simon had learned that the way to challenge llamas to a spitting contest was to stare hard at them. It seemed, for some reason, to annoy them. Now Mr. Crude was watching Simon out of the corner of his eye. He was waiting, Simon could tell, for the right moment to strike. As he sat, Simon rehearsed Uncle Philbert's advice.

"Use that gap in your front teeth," Philbert had told him. "Your orthodontist may hate it, but it's great for spittin'."

Simon was ready when Mr. Crude raised his head and drew a bead on him. Fixing the llama with a steady stare, Simon placed his tongue behind his front teeth, aimed in the direction of Mr. Crude, and spat as hard as he could.

This time, instead of the shotgun spray he usually produced, a big gob of spit shot from between Simon's teeth like a bullet. It hit Mr. Crude right on the nose. The llama couldn't have looked more surprised if Simon had flattened him with a fire hose. Simon laughed so hard that he fell off the fence.

From that day on, Simon was unbeatable. Soon the llamas edged nervously away when they saw him coming. Even Mr. Ugly knew that if he tried any funny stuff with Simon, he'd get it right between the eyes.

But as much as he liked the llamas, Simon spent most of his free time with Hero. Twice a day, he brought the chestnut horse his grain and hay. Mattie was happy to have him feed Hero, and after Simon had begged her enough times, she agreed to let Simon brush the horse, too.

"I never bothered with grooming him," she told Simon, leading him to a dusty tack box at the back of the stable. "I figured he didn't need people fussing over him and making his life a misery. What he needs is freedom. Besides, I was too worried about getting kicked. That horse doesn't trust people much, and who can blame him? Now, you keep clear of his back legs, and don't let him nip you."

Inside the box, Simon found curry combs and body brushes, hoof picks, oil, saddle soaps—everything for grooming a horse. Best of all, at the bottom of the box, was a tattered book, *You and Your Horse*. Here, Simon found advice and illustrations on everything to do with horse care and riding.

Simon knew better than to rush things with Hero. So for the first few days, he simply fed the horse, watching him over the top of the stall door and talking to him while the horse snuffed and blew and rolled his eyes up to watch the boy without lifting his head from the grain bin.

Every morning, Mattie would fill Simon's pockets with carrots. By the third day, when Simon arrived, Hero was waiting, his head resting on the door, looking for his treat. Simon played dumb: "What are you lookin' at me like that for, you silly beast?" The horse ducked his head and butted Simon in the chest, then started a snuffling search of his pockets.

"Okay, okay!" Simon laughed, producing the carrots and remembering to hold his hand flat to avoid the horse's teeth, the way it said to in the book. When Hero was done with the carrots, he thrust his head into Simon's neck and started chomping on the collar buttons of his shirt. His whiskers and soft skin tickled, but Simon held very still, so as not to startle him. Hero kept his

head there, against Simon's chest, while Simon found the spots by his ears that needed scratching, and Hero blew his hot breath into Simon's sweater and nibbled on buttons and tilted his ears forward to catch the flow of words that tumbled from Simon. And they stood like that for half an hour while Simon told Hero everything. He told him how much he admired him for bucking off his old owner. He told him that if he had anything to say about it, no one would ever hurt Hero again. He told him about himself, and about his mother and father. He told him about school and the other kids in his class, about Mrs. Biggs, his teacher, and about how he hoped spring vacation would never end. And about how he wanted Hero to let him brush him.

After four days, Simon decided the moment had finally come. He got out the grooming tools and slowly opened the stall door. Hero backed nervously away. Simon wondered if he should tie Hero's head with the halter hanging by the door. Instead, he kept up a steady stream of talk, trying to calm the horse as he looked him over.

Grooming Hero would be no small job. The horse hadn't been properly brushed in a year. His dull brown coat, thick and shaggy from the winter, was full of burrs and caked with mud. His tail and mane were snarled and filthy.

Simon leaned against Hero and, taking the rubber curry comb, started work on the matted, dirty coat. He worked slowly from head to tail, rubbing in circles, raising clouds of dust and horse hair as he went.

At first, Simon worried that Hero would get fed up, the way Simon used to when his mother had given *him* a haircut. But he soon discovered Hero's secret: the big lunk actually loved being brushed. The shivering and prancing, which had started when Simon first entered the stall, stopped the moment he laid a brush to Hero's neck. From time to time, the horse lifted his head off the stall door, turned to watch Simon at work, and nickered.

"What's the matter, you big dope?" asked Simon happily at these times. "Did I miss a spot or something?"

The job took Simon several hours. When he had finished currying, he tackled the mane and tail. The tail was so tangled, he could only comb it out a few inches at a time. Then, dipping the body brush in water, he worked on the snarled mane until it lay in neat black strands on Hero's neck. Next he took a soft cloth, wet it, and rubbed and polished Hero's whole body. He took a can of hoof oil from the tack box and brushed each of Hero's hooves with the shiny liquid. Last of all—studying the drawings in the book—he made a stab at braiding the tail. It didn't look nearly as fine as the tail of the horse in the illustration, but Simon had to admit it was pretty fantastic.

When it was all over, Simon was filthy, and exhausted. But the horse was transformed. The shaggy wild beast was gone. In his place was a sleek and shining animal. His chestnut coat shone like burnished metal. His polished hooves gleamed like black coal. And his dark mane shimmered in the light. Hero gave a great snort—almost a sigh—of happiness and laid his head over Simon's shoulder. And Simon stood there, loving the sheer weight of the animal and not wanting to move.

Finally, he pulled himself away.

"I'll be right back," he promised the horse.

Inside the farmhouse, he found Aunt Mattie sitting on

the couch, with several cats sleeping on her lap and shoulder.

"It's a beautiful day today, Simon," she said. "Would you like to play golf?"

"No," said Simon hastily. "I—"

"Good," said Mattie. "Neither would I."

It was only afterward that he realized that the old Simon would never have answered his aunt that way. But he didn't stop to think about it then.

"I've got something to show you. Come sit on the porch."

Mattie shooed Sugar off the porch, plucked a peacock out of her rocking chair, and did as she was told. Simon sprinted back into the barn. He grabbed the halter off the hook, slid it over Hero's head, and led him out of the barn, prancing excitedly—the horse, that is, not Simon.

When he came in sight of the porch, his aunt gasped and sat straight up in her chair.

"My dear, where did you get that absolutely divine horse?"

"That's Hero, Aunt Mattie."

"Never!" shouted Mattie. "Hero is a scruffy, filthy old rag. This—why, this creature is a gorgeous thoroughbred from some racetrack."

Simon laughed and rubbed Hero's neck. For his part, Hero bent down and ate one of Aunt Mattie's bright orange tulips.

Interrup –

The following day, Simon was helping Aunt Mattie feed the llamas. Just as Mattie was emptying some grain into their trough, one of the smaller ones leaned down and nipped her broad bottom. Mattie shrieked loudly and shook a finger at them.

"Miserable ingrates! Mangy, mucculent misfits! Have you no gratitude? Biting the hand that feeds you!"

"Bottom," said Simon seriously.

"What?"

"They didn't bite the *hand* that feeds them; they bit the *bottom*."

Mattie nearly burst, laughing at Simon's little joke. She liked it so much that she repeated it that night at dinner to Uncle Philbert. Philbert looked surprised. "I'm sure you ain't allowed to say the word *bottom* in your own house."

Simon looked down at his plate of peach pie. "I'm not," he said. Nor was he allowed to say *butt* or *bum*. He had to say *backside*, or, worse, *derrière*. "My parents say it's not a nice word."

To his surprise, Philbert fixed Simon with a stern look. "Simon," he said, "I been meanin' to talk to you about your language. There's some words we just won't tolerate in this house, and that's one of them."

Simon blushed a bright crimson. "I'm sorry. I won't ever say *bottom* again—" he started to say. But Philbert interrupted him.

"*Bottom*—heck. I ain't talkin' about *bottom*. You can say *bottom* till you're blue in the gills if you like."

"Then what word *do* you mean?"

"*Nice*," said Uncle Philbert, rolling his eyes and pulling at his hair. "I hate that word. How was your day?" he continued in a high voice. "Nice. How was the movie? Nice. I had a nice time. Did you have a nice time? We all had a nice time. Have a nice day. What does *nice* mean? Does it mean exciting? Or relaxing? Or profitable? Nice—hah!"

"I wonder . . . ," murmured Mattie. "Let's see what it actually means." She reached behind her chair to a dishwasher Simon had never noticed before and pulled out the bottom rack. It was full of books and pads and notebooks stacked like plates. The silverware holder was full of pens and pencils, scissors, rulers, and bottles of glue. Mattie noticed Simon's stare. "This is my desk," she explained simply. And then she added, "Make sure you never turn the dishwasher on by mistake someday."

She pulled a tattered red *Webster's Dictionary* from the front rack, found the page she wanted, and read: " 'Nice: (adjective) dissolute'—oh, that means *very* badly behaved! That's the first meaning. The next meaning is 'fussy, persnickety.' And the third meaning is 'skillful.' There you go. Think of *that* the next time you use the word *nice!*"

"Have a very badly behaved day," said Simon solemnly.

"Have a fussy day," said Uncle Philbert.

"Have a skillful day," added Aunt Mattie.

"And speaking of bad language," said Philbert to Simon as soon as they had all stopped giggling, "somebody really needs to teach you how to cuss."

Mattie looked surprised. "I thought *you* were teaching him how to cuss."

"I thought you were."

Simon grinned excitedly. "Are you going to teach me how to swear? Really?"

Philbert gave him a disgusted look. "Not *swear*, Mr. Mush for Brains. *Cuss.* Any moron can swear. But it takes real genius to cuss. Your aunt is a champion cusser."

"Thank you, Bert," said Mattie, looking modestly down at her plate. She smoothed her place mat. "You're not half-bad yourself."

"I don't understand," said Simon. "What's the difference between cussing and swearing?"

"Swearin'," said Philbert, as if explaining to a two-year-old, "is just usin' bad language—you know, the kind of garbage you hear every day from some loudmouth on the street who doesn't have any imagination. Cussin' . . . well, cussin' is an art. You ever hear your aunt Mattie talk to the llamas?"

"Yes."

"That's cussin'."

"Or," added Mattie, "the way your great-uncle here talks to the farm machines. That's cussing."

"I see," said Simon, trying to remember what Mattie had called the llamas. Mangy something misfits. Mucculent. "Mangy, mucculent misfits." What did that mean? He reached for the dictionary.

"Pass the cinnamon," said Philbert, taking a large bite of pie. Simon, his head in his book, passed the cinnamon shaker absentmindedly to Uncle Philbert.

Aunt Mattie did not keep salt and pepper shakers on the table like most people. Well, she did have salt and pepper shakers. But they didn't have salt and pepper in them. They had cinnamon and Parmesan cheese. Or brown sugar and chili powder. "Why on earth would anyone want to put crystals of salt or crushed pepper seeds on *all* their food *all* the time?" Mattie said in surprise once when Simon asked her about this. And, as usual, Simon could think of no reason why he should put pepper or salt on all his food and not cinnamon or cheese.

Had Simon been at home, his mother would have reminded him that it was not polite to read at the table, and he would have had to put the dictionary away. But at Aunt Mattie's, it was quite acceptable to read at mealtime. Frequently, whole meals would pass with the three of them deep in their own books. (Philbert was working his way through the *Encyclopaedia Britannica*; currently he was on *J*. Mattie was reading something called *Zen and the Art of Motorcycle Maintenance*. And Simon was reading everything he could put his hands on that had to do with horses.) Often one of them would read a favorite part out loud. They'd all laugh and then go back to their books.

"And while we're on the subject of language," said

Philbert, pushing away his pie plate and reaching for a bowl of Cheerios, "there's altogether too much Not Speakin' Before Bein' Spoken To goin' on."

"Excuse me?" asked Simon, looking up from the dictionary. He had just discovered that *mucculent* meant "slimy," and was thinking of lots of good ways to use it. "Isn't it bad manners to—"

"And," Aunt Mattie added, "there's entirely not enough Interrupting."

Uncle Philbert paused, his spoon of Cheerios halfway to his mouth.

"There she goes again," he said to Simon.

"What?"

"Interruptin'," said Uncle Philbert. "She is *always* interrup—"

"Am I?" said Mattie. "I never noticed."

"My mother says it's rude to interrupt," said Simon shyly.

"Well, once again, Simon, I can tell you that interrupting is all a matter of what you're used to," said his great-aunt, giving each of them a ferocious stare. "In some places, like England, people always interrupt one another. You see, if the conversation is interesting enough, people can't wait to start talking. It adds excitement.

"But in this country, for some strange reason, it's always considered rude. You have to wait till some old windbag is done repeating himself five or six times." She glared at Philbert. "And then, when you're sure it's safe, you may speak. In my humble opinion, it is far ruder to be the old windbag than to be the interrupter. Because by the time it's safe for anyone else to open his mouth, he's forgotten what he wanted to say. Or wandered off to talk to the cats."

"So interrupting is *not* rude?" asked Simon, unable to believe his ears.

"Well, sometimes it is," said Philbert, "and—"

"Sometimes it isn't," Mattie interrupted. She smiled at Simon. "Why don't you give it a try?"

"Me? Try interrupting?" Simon was shocked.

"Yes," said his aunt. "You need practice to unlearn old habits and learn some new ones."

"Give the boy a chance," said Uncle Philbert. "He's got to get used to the idea. Interruptin' is not a skill you can just pick up overnight."

It was true. It was one thing to be told it was okay to interrupt, for example. It was quite another to do it in real life. Over the next few days, Simon made an effort. Time after time, he failed. Then one evening at dinner, Uncle Philbert was telling a story about how he got kicked by a mule.

"Next thing you know," said Philbert, "that ornery critter curled his ugly lips back and—"

Simon saw an opening.

"Pass the cinnamon, please," he interrupted.

"Wrong!" said Philbert. "Rude!"

Simon looked bewildered.

"It shows you weren't listening to him," explained Mattie. "Now try again."

Philbert resumed the story.

"And the mule opened his mouth, and—"

"Once I saw a horse bite someone," said Simon, swinging (as it were) wildly.

"Wrong!" said Mattie and Philbert together. "That sounds like you can't wait to talk about *yourself*. If, for example, you interrupted to ask what color the mule's teeth were," Mattie explained patiently, "now *that* would be fine. It shows you are so interested in what he is saying, you can't wait to know more."

"Okay," said Simon. "I think I get it now. Try me again." He bent over his plate, concentrating hard. This time, he would do it right! He felt inspiration filling him. He breathed deeply and slowly.

"And after he planted his feet on my backside,"

Uncle Philbert concluded his story, "I pulled up my shirt, and danged if he hadn't kicked me so hard, there was the shape of his ornery hoof right there on my skin. Like a tattoo. Why, you could even count the nails in his h—"

"I hope you sold that no-good, hairy troglodyte to the glue factory!" Simon cried.

There was a moment's hush. Mattie and Philbert exchanged glances.

"Yes!" they said. Philbert looked awed. "Boy," he said solemnly, "first off, you interrupted beautifully—perfect timing, really perfect. And then you threw in a batch of really fine cuss words for good measure. Hang me if you ain't a prodigy. Prod-i-gy." Mattie gave him a second helping of pie. Philbert sat back, put his handkerchief to his lips, and burped. Simon jabbed his thumb into his forehead. He went happily around the table, giving everyone a playful punch in the arm.

He couldn't have done it at home. But he wasn't at home now, was he?

All Good Things Must End

Several nights later, Simon lay sprawled on the couch, enjoying the horsey smell that wafted off his clothes. Some people—his father for one—might have said he was being idle. (George Maxwell was never idle. He was always fixing storm windows or looking things up in dictionaries or making lists.)

Simon might have looked idle. But actually, he was thinking. He was thinking about burping. Despite all of Uncle Philbert's un-lessons, the one area in which Simon had made no progress at all was with the Gentle Art of Burping. "You ain't a proper kid," said Philbert, "unless'n you can burp."

Uncle Philbert was able to produce a burp at a moment's notice—long burps, short burps, delicate burps, disgusting burps. He coached Simon hour after hour: "It's all in the throat, my boy. You tighten up those throat muscles, you see, like this, and then suck in real hard.

Then let 'er rip. Be sure you cover your mouth, son. Ain't nobody wants to look at your tonsils when you're burpin'."

But Simon couldn't ever seem to manage more than a fake-sounding croak.

That night, he lay there on the couch, enjoying the horsey smell, and thought, If I could just learn to burp, then everything would be perfect.

At that very moment, the phone rang. Both Mattie and Philbert looked startled. Simon realized it was the first time the telephone had rung since he'd been there.

"Botheration," said Mattie, putting down her book. "You answer it, Bert. I've got a parrot on my shoulder." As indeed she did.

Philbert leaped up from his end of the couch and began rummaging under the piles of magazines. The phone continued ringing, making an oddly muffled sound.

"Now just where *is* that phone?" asked Philbert.

"Don't know, dear," said Mattie, looking around vaguely. "The last time I saw it, it was under that crate of cat food."

"Well, it's not there now," huffed Uncle Philbert. "Oh, the devil take it!" he said, sinking back onto the couch. At that moment, the phone rang one last time, and Philbert jumped up again. The telephone, in fact, was under the very sofa cushion he was sitting on. It was an old-fashioned phone, the kind with a heavy, curved receiver and a round metal dial. Philbert snatched up the receiver, holding it out between thumb and forefinger as if it were some particularly poisonous sort of viper.

"I already got one!" he shouted into it, and stuffed the machine back under the cushion. "It's probably just

someone trying to sell me a trip to Florida," Philbert explained. "I already been once. 1937. Didn't like it then, wouldn't like it now."

The phone rang again. This time, Mattie answered it, while Runcible teetered on her shoulder.

"Hell-ow!" she said. She had probably meant to say hello in the normal way, but as she opened her mouth, Runcible had dug her claws straight into Aunt Mattie's shoulder. And then, as the other person started to speak, Runcible leaned over and shouted into the phone, "Shut your trap!"

"Just a minute," said Mattie, trying to muzzle the parrot with one hand. "Simon, dear, it's for you."

It was Simon's mother. For a moment, neither one of them could think of anything to say. Simon was shocked to realize that he hadn't missed his mother or father once, after that first morning. Hadn't even thought about them. Now for an instant, he had trouble imagining what they looked like, where they were standing while they spoke on the phone, what day it was.

Simon's mother was speechless for different reasons. At last she said, "Simon? What was all that about? Hello? Simon?"

"Hello, Mother. . . . Oh, that? That was just Runcible. The parrot. . . . No, *that* was Uncle Philbert. He must have, um, thought it was a wrong number." As he spoke, Simon sat up straighter and straighter. "Of course I'm all right. Why wouldn't I be? Yes, Mother. . . . Yes, Mother. . . . Tomorrow. The ten o'clock train. See you then. . . . Yes. . . . Good-bye, Mother."

He hung up the phone and sat stunned for a few minutes.

"Going home?" asked Philbert.

Simon nodded dumbly. He couldn't even think about it.

"That must have been your mother, then," said Mattie briskly. "And how is she?"

"I don't know. We couldn't talk for long"—here Simon could not keep a slightly sarcastic note from creeping into his voice—"because it seems Aunt Bea and Uncle Fred are still there, and they were expecting an important call and we mustn't tie up the phone."

Mattie gave him a long glance. "You have to take the train tomorrow?"

"Yes."

"Well, time just flew, didn't it?"

Simon was silent.

"But you must be eager to get home?" asked his great-aunt gently.

At last he said, "Do I have to say the polite thing? Or the truth? Because the truth is, I don't want to go home. It's different here. I like it. Home is . . . Well, Aunt Bea and Uncle Fred are still there. Parker is still in my room. I'm going to have to sleep on the couch, I bet, while smelly old Parker messes up my room."

Simon kicked at a stack of old phone books as he talked—they were being used as a coffee table. Runcible fluttered up to the rubber tree on the ceiling.

"And I don't want to go back to school again. I hate Mrs. Biggs. And all the kids at school hate me. And . . ." As tears of self-pity filled his eyes, Simon got to his feet. "I'm going up to bed," he said. "Good-night." And he took the stairs two at a time.

It was only after he'd finished brushing his teeth that Simon realized what else had been bugging him about the conversation with his mother. She hadn't even bothered to ask after Uncle Philbert and Aunt Mattie. Not a word. As he lay in bed pondering this, there was a knock on the door, and Mattie came in.

"I know boys don't like to be kissed," she said, "but for once you have to be polite to your old auntie and let me give you a last good-night kiss."

She bent over quickly and kissed him on the forehead, and before she could straighten up, Simon grabbed her hand.

"There are two things I forgot to say," he said. "First, I forgot to say that the real reason I don't want to go home is because I had such a good time here—"

"I know that, Simon," said Mattie with a smile.

Simon took a deep breath. "And the other thing is that my mother sends her love."

Mattie stood looking at him for a spell, the smile still
lingering on her lips. Then she bent over and brushed the
hair out of his eyes. "Thank you for that little lie, my
dear."

And before Simon could say anything, she had gone.

Bad-bye

The next morning was miserable. As a special treat for breakfast, Uncle Philbert had made Simon his Twenty-Four-Alarm Chili and Beans ("guaranteed to fry your innards"). Stayed up all night letting it simmer, he did. But Simon had no appetite.

When Philbert saw he wasn't eating, he slapped him on the back.

"That's right, boy!" he said. "Never pretend you like someone's cookin' when you don't. Try eatin' something you hate and you'll lose your lunch all over the table. Nothing, *nothing*, is worse manners than barfing at the table."

Simon remembered what Philbert had taught him during the long lesson on Table Manners: never eat something you can't stand, but always thank the cook for going to the trouble.

"I love your chili, Uncle Philbert. You know I do. It's just . . . I don't feel hungry right now."

"Of course you don't," said Aunt Mattie. "Why don't you run along and get packed?"

So Simon got up from the table. He didn't say, "May I be excused?" because the first time he'd asked that, Philbert had nearly split himself from laughing. "Excused for what? Finishing your meal? Being alive?"

Instead of packing, however, he ran out to the paddock and climbed up on the fence. He put his fingers in his mouth and gave a shrill whistle. Hero looked up from the other side of the field and cantered over. He nearly knocked Simon over backward searching his pockets for carrots. While he chewed, Simon talked. Simon told him he was leaving. He might never see Hero again. He rubbed Hero's ears and told him there was one more thing he wanted to do before he left.

Simon jumped down, walked to Hero's side, and pushed the horse gently until his broad flank was against the fence. Then Simon mounted the fence. "I want you to let me ride you just once. Just for a moment. That's all," said Simon, talking gently into Hero's ear. The horse shuddered, lowered his head, and pawed at the ground. But he stayed put. Slowly, Simon lifted one leg and slid it partway across Hero's back. He let it rest there a moment while Hero got used to the feel of it. The horse was holding stock-still now, as if he sensed that Simon had never been on a horse before. Simon slid his whole weight onto Hero's back, clinging with one hand to the fence and keeping the other around Hero's neck. Then he let go of the fence, and he was sitting on Hero's back. Simon felt all the horse's muscles bunching under him, as if it was taking every ounce of Hero's strength just to hold still.

Trying hard to remember what the book had said

about riding, Simon nudged Hero with his heel, all the while talking quietly into his ear. Hero took a step forward alongside the fence, then another. When they were halfway around the paddock, Simon leaned forward and thrust his heels into Hero's side. The horse went straight from a walk into a long, slow canter. To Simon's own

amazement, he didn't slide off into the mud. Somehow he stayed up there, clinging to Hero's mane, until they had made a complete circle of the paddock. Hero slowed to a halt before the fence, and Simon slid off his back.

"It's our secret," said Simon. "No one will ever know." And then he gave him one last pat, and one last carrot, and went inside to pack.

Saying good-bye to Raspberry was almost as hard as saying good-bye to Hero. The cat jumped onto his bed while he folded his clothes, and rolled around on them, as if trying to stop Simon from packing. Each time Simon bent over his suitcase, Raspberry walked under him, his tail brushing Simon's face, his head turned to look into Simon's eyes, a loud purr rumbling in his chest. For an instant, Simon toyed with the idea of packing Raspberry in his suitcase, too. He hugged him to his head one last time, then darted downstairs.

Here, he said good-bye to Runcible ("Good-bye, good riddance," the parrot answered); and the peacocks, who were preening by the porch; and Sugar, who took one last lump; and Mr. Ugly, who exchanged one last spitball with him; and finally, Uncle Philbert, who said it would be real nice to have his sofa back, thanks very much, and to be sure to remember to write a thank-you note, hardy-har-har.

They were, of course, late getting to the station, but not late enough, for the train was also late. Simon and Mattie stood silently, neither one feeling much like making up polite conversation, until Simon heard the train approaching.

Then he turned to his great-aunt and, speaking quickly, said, "Aunt Mattie, why is it that my family doesn't like you? I used to think it was because you were a witch."

"Really?" said Mattie, a gleam of humor in her eyes. "Tell me, what do they say about me?"

"They don't say anything—that's just the problem. They say you're 'you know.' What do they mean by that?"

She laughed and handed him a package. "Here's some lunch for you. A piece of lemon meringue pie. And for dessert, a pickle sandwich."

The train had pulled into the station. Mattie folded Simon in that hug she had, the one that smelled of licorice and lavender, and picked up his suitcase. She bustled him onto the train. But he turned to look at her from the steps as the train pulled out.

"What do they mean?" he demanded.

"Didn't anyone teach you not to ask so many questions?" Mattie laughed. She waved and blew him a kiss.

Be Nice

His mother was waiting for him as the train pulled in, an anxious expression on her face. She looked as if she'd been there a long time. Poor Mother, thought Simon, realizing as he did so that he'd never felt that particular emotion before. She gave him a long hug, rumpled his hair, smoothed it down again.

"How brown you are! You look so . . . different. Did you have a nice time? Gracious, whatever happened to your shirt?"

"Oh, that's just llama spit. You see, the Stain Remover only kind of spread it a—"

"Llama spit! And the buttons are all missing!"

"Oh, Hero, the horse, ate them. You see—"

Mrs. Maxwell covered her ears. "I don't think I want to know *any* more. You poor boy. Thank goodness you're home safe and sound."

Simon sighed. "I'm sorry I'm late—" he began. And then he stopped. "No, I'm not. You should do what Aunt

Mattie does. Try being a little late all the time. It makes things more interesting."

"What?" asked his mother.

"Like, well, what did you do while you were waiting for me?"

"Do? I checked the timetable. I paced. I looked at my watch."

Simon realized that this wasn't going to be as easy as he'd thought.

"I don't know what Aunt Matilda has been telling you, Simon, but being late shows a lack of respect. It's just plain rude."

"But—"

"I hope I won't have any of that around Aunt Bea and Uncle Fred."

"No, Mother."

He threw his duffel into the back of the old station wagon.

"Where's Father?" he asked. He thought his father might have come to the station to meet him.

"He wanted to be here, but his boss—you know, Mr. Hackney—called and asked him to attend a special meeting. He won't get home till after you're in bed, I'm afraid."

"On a *Sunday*?"

"Yes, I know, it's unfair, but he's working very hard to get this promotion. He's made up a very clever ad campaign for the chewing-gum magnate."

"What is it?"

"Well, he wants to call the gum Dubble Bubble. And the ad shows some witches stirring a pot, and all sorts of bubbles are coming out, and they're singing this jingle: 'Double, double toil and trouble; Fire burn and . . .

Dubble Bubble.' It comes from a Shakespeare play. The client is going to love it."

Simon laughed. "It's good."

"Yes, even Uncle Fred and Aunt Bea thought it was funny."

Simon's smile turned to a frown. "Why are Uncle Fred and Aunt Bea still here?" he asked. "You promised they would only stay two weeks."

"Now, dear, I know it's exasperating, but imagine how they must feel—their kitchen still isn't done; the workmen are way behind schedule. They can't move back in with the place full of plaster dust and no stove or water, can they?"

"Does this mean I get to sleep on the couch? And horrible, fat old Parker is still in my room?"

"Simon!" Her voice was shocked. "I won't have you talking that way about your own cousin." Then she softened. "I know it's hard for you. But what else can we do? We can't ask them to leave. And it will only be for another week or so. And you mustn't call him 'fat old Parker.' He's slightly overweight, but that's not his fault. It's genetic."

"A *week*, Mother? I can't bear it for that long! It's not fair. Why don't they go stay in a hotel, like we did when our house was being done over?"

"Well, I . . ." But his mother seemed to have no answer to this question. "We just can't ask them to leave," she said. "And that's all there is to it. Here we are. There's Aunt Bea. Now remember to shake their hands. And be nice and polite."

Simon did shake hands with Aunt Bea, thankful that he didn't have to kiss her.

"Hello, Aunt Bea. Yes, the train trip was fine. Yes, it was a little late."

Aunt Bea was a tall, big-toothed woman with extremely red hair. Her voice, while not exactly loud, had a piercing quality to it that meant it traveled. Simon guessed there would be no room in their small house that would be out of range of her voice. He remembered his mother saying that Aunt Bea really didn't like children, and that was another reason for Simon to be away while she was here.

"You've grown very tall," said Aunt Bea with a "let's get this over with" kind of tone in her voice. "I'm sure you had a nice time in the country."

"Very nice," mumbled Simon. "Very dissolute."

"Good. Don't mumble," said his aunt, already turning away to talk to his mother. "Now, Shirley, when is the cleaning woman coming? Parker's asthma is really acting up, and I'm sure it's because of all the dust."

His mother laughed nervously. "I'm such a terrible housekeeper," she said.

At that moment, Uncle Fred appeared. A large man with very red cheeks, he shook Simon's hand, and then, with the air of having made a major discovery, told him that he had grown.

Simon admitted that this was probably true, and then, when it was clear that Uncle Fred had run out of conversation, Simon took the opportunity to escape to his room. He flung open the door with relief.

"Hey!" said a voice from the bed. "Don't you know it's rude to barge into somebody's room without knocking?"

It was Parker. The chubby older boy was curled up in a

sleeping bag on Simon's bed. He was in his pajamas and was reading Simon's comics. Simon's jaw dropped in disbelief—not because Parker had pilfered his beloved comic book collection, but because of the room. It was

totally bare. Gone were the curtains and rug, the books and bookshelves, the model airplanes, the rock collection, the goldfish bowl, the Pirates banners, the Wayne Gretzky posters, the stuffed armchair. Nothing was left but a stripped bed, a barren desk, and a tiny TV set.

"Where's all my stuff?" yelled Simon.

"In storage," said Parker, not bothering to look up from his comic—or rather, Simon's comic. He pulled a handful of Cheesios from a bag beside him and stuffed them in his mouth. "Took your mom a whole day to do it," he said, spraying little Cheesio crumbs over the sheets as he spoke.

"Why? Why is it in storage?"

"Because of my asthma, you know," said Parker. "Too much dust in here. We had to scrub the whole room, and all your stuff was in the way. Dust magnets, most of it. Made me cough." He gave Simon a wicked smile, and produced a little fake wheeze to show what he meant. "Oh, don't worry, you'll get it back when I leave. And I saved out your X-Men collection." He lifted a pillow to show Simon a stack of comics, his precious comics, all rumpled and torn, their covers coming off.

What Simon wanted to do was to murder Parker. He wondered briefly if it was against the law to kill someone who had destroyed your comic book collection. He wanted to say, "Get off my bed! Get out of my room!"

Instead, he stood speechless for several moments, watching Parker eat, and then turned on his heel and left the room.

"Oh, and Simon," Parker called after him, "bring me another bag of Cheesios from the kitchen, wouldja?"

82

"Mother, can I ask you something?" said Simon. She was helping him arrange a sleeping bag on the foldout living room couch, which was to be his bed for who knows how long.

"I know what you're going to say, Simon. You don't like Parker, and you don't like sleeping on the couch. But Parker can't sleep out here because of the dust. There's nothing to be done about it. You must be polite to him."

"No. I was going to ask you if you like having Aunt Bea and Uncle Fred here."

"Why, of course! Fred's your father's brother. I love him."

"But do you *like* having them stay with us?"

"It's a little awkward and inconvenient, all of us having to go to bed at nine o'clock so you can sleep in the living room, but, well—"

"Do you like Aunt Bea?"

"Of course I do! Why shouldn't I? She can be a little, um, loud—"

"And bossy and rude."

"Simon! Lower your voice. She might hear you. You must not talk about your aunt that way."

"Why not?"

"Well, because—" His mother broke off and stared hard at him. "Simon Maxwell, I have never heard you speak this way before. You used to be so well behaved. Where are your manners? Is this Matilda's doing? What on earth has she been filling your head with? Oh, I knew I shouldn't have let you go there. I knew it! Fred was right."

"No, Mother, you're wrong. I had a wonderful time.

And I learned all about manners." He climbed into his sleeping bag. "Someday I'll tell you all about it."

His mother looked doubtful. Then she smoothed his hair and bent to kiss him. "All right, Simon. As long as you mind your manners while they're here."

"Yes, Mother."

"Get some sleep. School tomorrow. And it's a big day for you."

Simon frowned. "Why?"

"Simon! Tomorrow's your birthday! Did you forget?"

Simon's head sank back into the pillow. "My birthday. I almost forgot." He had hardly thought of it at all at Aunt Mattie's. There was an awkward pause.

"I know it's late, but would you like me to invite anyone special?" His mother wore an anxious look. Birthday parties were always a problem for Simon. He never got asked to other kids' parties, and he'd given up asking them to his.

"No," he said slowly. Then he had an idea. It popped into his mind at that instant, fully formed, like a turtle hatching from an egg. It was the solution to everything. "Wait—yes. There *is* someone I want you to ask." He sat up in bed. "Aunt Mattie and Uncle Philbert."

"Oh no, Simon," his mother answered, clearly taken aback. "We can't do that."

"Why not?"

"Well, because . . . because they live too far away. And because Aunt Bea and Uncle Fred—"

"It's not far by car," answered Simon. "Please!"

"I just don't know, Simon. I'll have to think about it. Good-night."

"Good-night," said Simon. Mrs. Maxwell left and

Simon thought about his cousin, sleeping in Simon's room on Simon's bed. "Bad-night to you, Parker." Then, remembering his training, he added, "You overinflated landlubber." He smiled. Uncle Philbert would have liked that.

Very Discombobulate

On the morning of his birthday, Simon walked into the kitchen, where his mother labored by the stove.

His father was on the phone. Simon could tell he was talking to his boss, Mr. Hackney.

"Yes, sir, I'd be happy to, sir. No problem." He saw Simon and smiled, silently mouthing the words *Good morning*.

Simon mouthed *Good morning* back to him and turned to his mother.

"And how does your corporosity seem to gashiate today?" he asked.

"Could you pass me that oven mitt?" asked his mother. "Gosh, I've burned these. Oh, good morning, Simon," she added, as if she'd just seen him. "Happy birthday. I'm afraid we're out of Rice Poppies." She glanced at the kitchen table, where Parker sat eating a large bowl of Simon's favorite cereal. Parker made a sad face and shook the empty box of Rice Poppies.

"Sorry, old boy." He smiled.

"That's okay, Mother. I'll have pizza."

That got his mother's attention. "You'll do no such thing!" she said. "I'll make you some oatmeal."

"Okay," said Simon with a sigh, adding to himself, "Very discombobulate, great congruity, dissimilarity." Suddenly, he thought of something. "Mother, did you remember to invite Aunt Mattie and Uncle Philbert?"

"Well now, Simon, I just couldn't." She glanced toward Uncle Fred and Aunt Bea and put a finger over her lips. "It wouldn't work out with, you know," she whispered, cocking her head toward the relatives. "They wouldn't get along." She handed Simon his bowl of oatmeal. He took it without a word.

Breakfast was a silent affair, because Uncle Fred was reading Mr. Maxwell's newspaper, and he needed complete quiet for this ritual.

Mr. Maxwell watched Uncle Fred from the kitchen, where he was still tied to the phone. He was fuming—but silently. Simon knew his father hated to have his newspaper pulled apart before he'd had a chance to read it, and that's just what Uncle Fred was doing. He'd even ripped out an article called "You and Your Home Equity Loan" that he apparently found interesting, leaving a gaping hole in the comics page Simon had planned to read. Simon could see his father's face grow red. His mother, meanwhile, was frantically preparing three different breakfasts for their visitors—oatmeal for Uncle Fred, more cereal and toast for Parker, and eggs and bacon for Aunt Bea.

"Good morning, Uncle Fred," said Simon.

"Mmm," grunted Uncle Fred without looking up.

"And how does your corporosity seem to gashiate?"

asked Simon, who began carrying on a little conversation with himself. "Very discombobulate? Oh, really? That's good. And it's your birthday, too? Oh, happy birthday, Simon. Thank you. No, really. Not at all."

Uncle Fred looked at him over the top of the newspaper. He frowned slightly.

"Simon, I'm surprised at you. Your father and I were

brought up to believe that children should be seen and not heard."

Simon sighed and found himself thinking wistfully of Uncle Philbert's Twenty-Four-Alarm Chili; if he had it now, he'd substitute it for the oatmeal Uncle Fred was blindly eating behind his newspaper. Give him a real surprise!

But Simon ate his oatmeal quietly. He thought back to the last time Uncle Fred and Aunt Bea had visited. He had smiled and sat with them in the living room and told them how happy he was at school, and that yes, he certainly *was* looking forward to having a chance to spend some time with Parker. And he thanked them for the "nice" stationery they gave him for Christmas ("So you can write *us* thank-you letters, pah-hah-hah!" his aunt had said with her explosive, braying laugh). And later Simon had sat at his desk and carefully written a two-page thank-you letter for the stationery. And Parker had played with Simon's favorite Christmas present, despite Simon's pleas to leave it alone, and had broken it, then laughed when Simon was upset. And Simon had covered up for Parker and told his parents he had broken it himself and then of course had gotten in trouble.

From the kitchen, he could hear Aunt Bea discussing cleaning with his mother. She was giving Mrs. Maxwell precise instructions on the right and wrong way to remove dust from rugs and curtains.

"Simon, dear," said his mother as he placed his unfinished oatmeal in the sink, "have you tidied the living room? The cleaning woman is coming soon and—there she is!" His mother hastened to answer the door. "Oh, Doris, come right in. Here, let me take your hat."

Doris was a large and frowning woman. Simon had never seen her smile, and his mother seemed to live in terror of her. Doris looked all around her as Mrs. Maxwell took her coat and hat, her gaze coming to rest on the visiting relatives.

"Large crowds still here, I see," she said with that note of disapproval in her voice. "Large crowds make lots of dirt."

"Yes, Doris."

"Lots of dirt makes lots of work for Doris."

"Yes, well, I've been tidying today, so . . ." His mother's voice trailed off. For the first time, Simon wondered if all mothers went around the house cleaning up before the cleaning lady came. Once, he'd even seen his mother scrubbing the toilet because it was "too dirty," even, apparently, for the cleaning lady to clean.

Doris went grumpily about her work, with Aunt Bea trailing behind and giving instructions, all of which Doris ignored. Mr. Maxwell came into the kitchen with his briefcase. He hadn't had time to eat breakfast or read the paper. As Mrs. Maxwell gathered up Aunt Bea and Uncle Fred's dishes, she paused to kiss him good-bye, saying cheerily, "When will you be home, dear?"

"I'll miss dinner," said Mr. Maxwell. "Mr. Hackney has asked me to work late all this week. I have no choice."

"But, George, you haven't seen Simon for two weeks, and it's his birthday today! You can't miss that. We're going to have a little party. I'm making tacos, his favorite meal."

Mr. Maxwell looked stricken. "Our biggest client is flying in from Ohio tonight. Dubble Bubble chewing gum. I'm supposed to take him to dinner and make my big presentation. You remember, 'Double, double toil and trouble.'"

Simon said nothing.

"Damn. Simon, I'm terribly sorry."

Simon stared at the ground. His father never swore. He must really be sorry. But Simon couldn't imagine a birthday party without his father.

"That's okay, Father," he said finally, without looking up. "I don't mind. Really."

Aunt Bea chose this moment to interrupt. "Oh, I'm afraid Uncle Fred can't eat tacos," she said. But Simon thought she didn't really sound afraid of anything. "Spicy foods don't agree with him. And that roughage, he can't have roughage."

This seemed as good a time as any for Simon to make his escape. He left the kitchen without saying good-bye. But instead of heading for the door—he was already late for the bus—he darted into his room, or rather, the living room. He picked up the phone and, as quietly as possible, started dialing. It rang and rang, and Simon prayed someone would answer. Finally, after about twenty rings, the phone was picked up.

"Hello?" said Simon.

"Don't want any," snapped a gruff voice.

Simon smiled.

Simple Simon

Simon dashed out the door without saying good-bye and headed for the bus stop. He had almost reached it when he heard footsteps coming quickly up behind him. Instinctively, Simon started running; if it was Peters and Shapiro, he figured, he could get to the relative safety of the bus stop before they caught him.

"Hey, Simon, wait up." It was Parker, puffing and bright red. "You're supposed to take me to the bus stop, dork."

Of course. Parker was going to have to ride Simon's bus, and Simon had been told to show him where to wait for it. His cousin gave him a rough cuff on the head, the kind of painful gesture that he often pretended was "just playing."

"Where are your manners, you dweeb."

"I'm sorry, I forgot," mumbled Simon. Though his cousin went to the same school, he was older and had classes in a different building. The two usually never saw each other at all during the day, which was fine with Simon.

As they rounded the corner, he saw he had been wrong about Peters and Shapiro. They weren't behind him. They were ahead of him—already waiting at the bus stop. Simon slowed down and prayed the bus would come soon.

"Who's your fat friend?" asked Peters. The older of the two boys, he was already a foot taller than Simon.

"Hey, Simple Simon met a pie man," snickered Shapiro, and the two boys guffawed at their wonderful joke. Simon was used to the teasing and ignored it, but he looked at Parker, expecting his cousin to respond. After all, Shapiro and Peters were big, but so was Parker. Instead, Parker flushed and turned his back on the pair. Parker had inherited his mother's red hair, and when he turned red, he really turned red. Though his back was

turned, Simon could see he had pulled out his asthma inhaler and was trying to breathe into it without anyone noticing.

Just then the bus arrived, and the two older boys shoved their way on board, followed by Simon and Parker. Simon knew enough to watch out for the legs that were always thrust into the aisle to trip him, but Parker didn't. When his cousin went sprawling onto the floor, Simon looked away, praying that Parker would not sit next to him.

He had known that Parker would make his life miserable at home. But it had never crossed his mind that Parker could add to his miseries at school this way. Yet another thing to be teased about. When the kids on the bus started chanting beneath their breath, he couldn't tell this time if they were saying "Simon, Simon" or "Pie man, pie man." Did it matter?

Toil and Trouble

DETENTION NOTICE:
NAME. Simon.
DATE. 5/12
TEACHER Mrs. Biggs
REASON Rude and
disrespectful.

When Simon got on the bus to go home after school that day, he was filled with a calm, happy feeling. Which was really strange, considering that the reason for that feeling was a pink detention slip in his back pocket—the first detention slip of his life.

He was feeling so calm and happy that he didn't even notice that no one tried to trip him when he got on the bus. He hardly noticed when Parker sat down beside him and the kids started chanting "Pie man, pie man."

"What's with you?" asked Parker. "You look like you won the lottery or something."

"Yeah, well, I got a detention," said Simon, and he couldn't help grinning.

"Why's that so great? Are you crazy? What'd you get it for?"

Simon thought a moment. "For not taking any guff, I guess."

"Huh?"

Simon gave Parker a quick rehash of the scene with Mrs. Biggs. Simon had been daydreaming, the way he always did in math class. He was so good at math that he never needed to pay much attention, the answers just kind of came to him. He'd been thinking about Raspberry and Hero when he heard Mrs. Biggs start lighting into Jimmy Bennett. She was talking in that sarcastic way she had, making fun of Jimmy for not being able to do the problem she'd written on the board.

"So I just interrupted her—didn't even raise my hand or anything—and told her she was wrong and Jimmy was right. It's true. Jimmy had the right answer. I don't know why I did it. It just kind of came out of my mouth before I could think."

"So what happened?"

"Her jaw dropped about a mile and a half. Then she told me I was rude and disrespectful. And she sent me to the principal's office. I had to sit in the red chair in the hall. I wish you could've seen her face."

"Oh, man, I hate that red chair."

Simon didn't answer him. He was thinking of the way all the kids in his class had smiled at him, given him a thumbs-up, or even—like Jimmy—a high five when they walked past him sitting in the hall there.

But Parker's next comment wiped the dreamy smile off Simon's face and made him sit up. "Your butt is gonna be in a sling when *you* get home," he said. "Whenever I bring home a detention slip, my dad fries me."

Simon didn't have time to think about this problem, for the bus was at their stop. As the cousins headed for the steps, Simon saw Peters and Shapiro coming up in back of them. He reached a hand for the railing just as a foot hooked his ankle. Simon pitched down the steps, grabbing the railing at the last minute. But he collided heavily with Parker, knocking him out the door.

"Whoops," said Peters loudly, for the benefit of the bus driver. "Gosh, are you okay?" As soon as the doors closed behind them and the yellow bus pulled away, Peters and Shapiro began laughing. "Golly gee," they repeated, with mock sympathy, "are you poor little boys okay?"

"Let's go," said Simon urgently to Parker. They set off at a trot, but the older boys were right behind them.

"Simple Simon!" yelled Peters.

"Hey, pie man," yelled Shapiro.

"Ignore them," hissed Simon to Parker, picking up his pace. "Come on, *run*."

He broke into a run, but beside him Parker was bright red, breathing with difficulty and patting his pockets for his inhaler.

"Can't you go any faster?"

"No," gasped Parker.

Simon slowed down, grabbed Parker by the elbow, and began propelling him forward. It was useless. The older boys caught up to them.

"Don't you know it's rude to walk away when someone's talking to you?" shouted Shapiro. Simon kept going, pushing Parker along in front of him.

Suddenly, a hand caught Simon by the shoulder and spun him roughly around. It was Peters. Before Simon knew what was happening, he was on the ground, with Peters astride him, Simon's hands pinned to the ground. Peters laughed as Simon struggled to throw him off. It was no use. The older boy was much heavier, much stronger. Simon was helpless.

Shapiro looked on, smirking. Parker was nowhere to be seen.

"Get off me," said Simon angrily. Peters was so heavy on his chest, Simon could hardly breathe, and the words came out as a rasp.

"Make me." Peters laughed. "Hey, Shapiro, lookit me— I'm a cowboy." He pumped up and down on Simon's chest, pretending to ride a horse. "Lookit my horse. Giddyap, horse."

"Get off," begged Simon.

"Say 'Uncle,' little horsie," said Peters, bouncing harder.

Simon felt like his ribs were cracking. He opened his mouth to say "Uncle," but in that moment he thought of Hero. And Uncle Philbert. And with the last bit of breath in his body, he lifted his head up as high as he could and waited until Peters was grinning down at him.

"Say 'Unc—' "

Simon let fly the biggest gob of spittle he could manage.

It hit Peters square in the eye.

Peters yelped and jumped up, dabbing at his eye and making disgusted noises. He turned to Simon, full of wrath. But Simon had scrambled to his feet, and before Peters could open his mouth, Simon launched another gob of spit, beautifully aimed. This one flew a distance of several feet and hit Peters just as squarely in the other eye.

Then Simon walked up to Peters. He stuck his face into the older boy's face, the way he'd seen his aunt Mattie do to the llamas when she was preparing to chew them out good and proper.

"You," he said slowly, "are a flocculent, flea-bitten, goat-faced, son-of-a-sea-slug." Then he turned his back on him and walked deliberately away. Though he was terrified, Simon refused to hurry his steps.

A noise from behind made Simon turn. He clenched his fists, ready for anything. But the two bullies weren't chasing him—weren't even looking at him.

Shapiro was standing by Peters, pointing at him and shaking with helpless laughter.

" 'Son-of-a-sea-slug,' " he repeated, gasping for breath. "That was good, Peters. You *are* kinda goat-faced, you know. And when he got you, splat, right in the eye—"

Peters gave Shapiro a shove in the chest that landed him in the dust. Shapiro sat there, still shaking with laughter. Soon the two were scuffling and rolling in the dirt.

Simon walked on.

Parker came out from behind a lilac bush, where he had apparently been hiding the whole time.

"Hey," he said, in a different voice than Simon had heard him use before. "That was so awesome. How'd you learn to spit and cuss like that?"

Simon looked at his cousin, thinking, The jerk ditched me. Saw I was in trouble and ran off and hid. Simon tried to feel angry at Parker. But it was no good. All he could feel for him was pity.

"Oh, it's nothing," said Simon, managing at least to put a little bit of scorn into his voice. "Just some ruderies my aunt and uncle taught me."

"Your aunt—you mean *my* mother and father?" Parker was shocked. Simon had to laugh at the thought of Aunt Bea and Uncle Fred cussing.

"No, Great-aunt Mattie and Uncle Philbert. That's how they talk to the llamas. And they have a parrot with the foulest mouth in the world."

"Wow. What a great aunt and uncle."

"They're your great-aunt and great-uncle, too."

"Maybe I can go visit them someday. Naw, that would never happen. Not in a million years would my parents let me visit. I'm surprised yours did."

Simon considered Parker for a moment. Having Uncle Fred and Aunt Bea for your parents must be pretty unbearable—even worse than having them for your aunt and uncle.

"They only let me go because we had to make room for you. I mean—" Simon stopped, aware of how his words sounded. He found himself feeling sorry for Parker, not wanting to hurt his feelings. This was absurd! He loathed Parker. Didn't he?

"Yeah, well, I guess it is a pain, having me in your room."

"Kind of," he admitted.

"Listen, could you teach me to spit like that? And cuss?"

Simon thought for a moment. "All right," he said. "But I want to sleep in my own room again."

"No sweat," said Parker. "You can have the bed. I'll sleep on the floor."

"And I want my comic books back."

"All right. I'll even throw in the Spider-Man one that I just bought. Deal?"

"Deal," said Simon, laughing. He turned and punched Parker in the arm—just hard enough.

Carrot Cake and Spinach Pasta

CHOCOLATE MARBLE

RED FROSTING

"It's lovely the way the boys get on so well together, isn't it?" Aunt Bea was saying to Mrs. Maxwell. She was helping frost the cake for Simon's party. "I've always said they were more like best friends than cousins. And it must be wonderful for Simon to have his older cousin around, to look after him on the bus and so on. Someone to look up to and admire, like a big brother."

"Mmm, yes, mustn't it?" said Mrs. Maxwell brightly. As she couldn't think of anything more to say on the subject, she added, "Um, don't you think red icing for the edges?"

"No, no, dearest," said Aunt Bea a bit sadly, as if to a hopelessly stupid four-year-old. "Red food coloring contains dyes that cause hyperactivity and hives. For Parker, that is. And they are very bad for everyone in general."

"But it's Simon's favorite color."

"A pity. He must learn to like green, then."

"Yes. Green. Well, I'm sure you're right."

"Of course I am! I'm—oh, here comes the birthday boy. Get out of the kitchen, you naughty boy—not allowed to see your cake till suppertime!"

Simon laughed and hid his eyes.

"Okay," he said. "Just tell me—chocolate marble cake with red frosting, right?"

"Um, well, not exactly," said his mother with a nervous laugh.

"What do you mean?" asked Simon. "That's what you always make for my birthday! It's my favorite."

"Yes, and very bad for you, too," Aunt Bea chimed in. "No sir, today we're having carrot cake with green frosting."

"*Carrot* cake?"

"Yes, full of vitamin C. No added sugar or artificial flavors. Extremely healthful. And instead of tacos—really,

103

Shirley, I don't know how you can feed your family such junk food—we're having spinach pasta with whole-wheat bread and sun-dried tomatoes."

"Carrot cake? Spinach pasta?" Simon was reeling. He shot his mother a look that said, *How could you?* And she sent back a pleading look that said very clearly, *Be nice. Please.*

Simon trudged into the living room and sat glaring out the window. What was the matter with his mother and father? he wondered. Why wouldn't they stand up for him? His mother let Aunt Bea ruin his party. His father wouldn't tell the boss he needed to be home for his own son's birthday.

"How many shall I set the table for?" asked Aunt Bea in the kitchen.

"Well, let's see, three of you and two of us makes—"

"Seven," said Simon, staring out the window with a huge grin on his face.

"No, dear, I wish you wouldn't interrupt like that. Three plus two makes five—"

"Seven." Simon pointed out the window, his grin growing even bigger.

There, pulling up into the Maxwells' driveway, was Aunt Mattie's ancient black car. Uncle Philbert was in the passenger seat. The goldfish bowl was on the dashboard. Raspberry sat between Mattie and Philbert, his front feet on the dashboard, his eyes on the fish. And Runcible perched on Mattie's broad hat.

That Dreadful Woman

Simon darted out of the house and up to the car just as Mattie heaved herself out of the door.

"Aunt Mattie!" he cried, and ran into her arms. "You came! I knew you'd come."

"Mind the parrot, my dear," said Mattie, dabbing at her hair, which, as usual, was escaping from several large hairpins beneath an enormous hat decorated with fruit. She was wearing a geranium-colored dress. "Oh, blastify these hairpins. Am I late?" Runcible hopped down to Simon's shoulder and promptly bit him on the ear.

"No—ow! No, you're right on time."

"Oh, dear. I'm afraid that's because I left my watch at home. Runcible, behave yourself, you contumelious creature. Come to Mama." Runcible walked back onto Mattie's finger and then to her shoulder, where she began chewing the fruit that bedecked Mattie's hat.

From the doorway, Bea and Mrs. Maxwell watched the scene in the driveway. Mrs. Maxwell's face was a picture of dismay.

"That dreadful woman!" exclaimed Aunt Bea. "Who invited *her*?"

"Not me. I mean, not I," stammered Mrs. Maxwell, who, even in distress, strove for correct grammar.

The passenger door opened, and Uncle Philbert climbed from the car.

"Don't say hello to your great-uncle or anything," he grumped. Simon detached himself from Aunt Mattie and went over to give him a hug. "Humph. Didn't anyone ever teach you any manners?"

"Not likely," said Simon. He pulled away from his uncle, lowered his chin to his chest, and burped—or pretended to—then jabbed himself in the forehead and punched his uncle on the arm.

"Still faking it, I see," said Philbert sadly. "Boy, when are you going to learn that it's all in the throat muscle—"

"But I am getting good at interrupting," said Simon, laughing.

"Well, Simon," said Mattie, pulling a large bag out of the car, "I see that your corporosity is gashiating nicely. Here, we've got lots of presents for you. But we mustn't stand here yammering. Where are your manners? Invite us in. I'd love to see your father—haven't seen him since he was a boy. And I've never met your mother—"

"Father's not here," said Simon quickly.

"What?" Mattie's eyebrows shot up. "Missing your birthday? Must be something *awfully* important."

"It's a chewing-gum magnate from Ohio," Simon explained. "A very important client. He's taking him out to dinner tonight."

"Oh, I see. A pity. Well, then, let's get these things inside and get down to business."

The three started for the door, but just at that moment a large black limousine pulled into the driveway behind them. Simon's father climbed out of the backseat and sprinted up to them.

"Simon! We were passing by on the way to the restaurant and I convinced Mr. Hackney to stop off so I could wish you a happy birthday. We're in a terrible hurry. I've only got a second." He glanced anxiously back at the limousine and then seemed to notice Mattie and Philbert for the first time. "What's all this?"

"This, Father, is Great-aunt Mattie and Uncle Philbert. They've come for my birthday." His father looked dumbstruck. "*I* invited them."

There was a whirring sound from the limo as one of the tinted windows was lowered. Mr. Hackney stuck his head outside. He was talking on the car phone. Simon could see another man in a dark suit sitting beside him. He must be the chewing-gum magnate, the very important client from Ohio. Mr. Dubble Bubble himself.

"Make it quick, Maxwell," said Mr. Hackney. He went back to his phone and whirred the window up.

"Yes, sir," said Mr. Maxwell to the tinted window. And then to Simon: "I'm really sorry to miss your party, son." He turned to Mattie and Philbert. For a moment, Simon saw his eye take in Philbert's faded farm clothes, Mattie's fruity hat, her geranium dress, the parrot, the decrepit car. He glanced nervously toward the limo, then stuck out a hand. "Aunt Mattie, Uncle Philbert. Wonderful to see you again," he said politely. He turned back to Simon and put his hands on his son's shoulders. "Well, Simon, I want you to have a very happy—"

There was another whir.

"Hurry it *up*, Maxwell!"

Whir.

A brief silence. Then Mattie walked over to the limousine and knocked on the window. It whirred open, and Hackney's exasperated face was visible. Mattie bent over and peered around the limo with undisguised curiosity. Then she smiled sweetly, opened her mouth, and said, "Say please!"

There was a stunned silence. Simon, who recognized Runcible's voice, closed his eyes. He wasn't sure he could watch this.

"I beg your pardon?" asked Mr. Hackney in a whisper.

"Say please," said Runcible once again, in a loud, clear voice. And then she added, "Dog breath!"

Simon's father gasped and turned pale, but Aunt Mattie nodded approvingly to Hackney. "I'm sure you meant to say please, didn't you? As in '*Please* hurry it up, Mr. Maxwell.' Though I hasten to add that you don't really have dog breath."

"Maxwell, what is the meaning of this?" called Mr. Hackney, his face a dangerous plum color. Beside him, Mr. Dubble Bubble was staring in fascination as Uncle Philbert approached the car.

"I don't know, sir. I've never met this woman before in my life."

Simon couldn't believe his ears. "Father!" he said. But his father wouldn't look at him.

At that moment, Uncle Philbert stuck out his hand.

"Howdy," he said to Mr. Hackney. "I'm Uncle Philbert."

Hackney glared at Simon's father. "We're wasting time!" he hissed. Then he looked at Uncle Philbert. "How d' you do?" he muttered quickly.

"What?" said Uncle Philbert.

"I said, 'How do you do?'" Hackney repeated with an air of disbelief, as if talking to an idiot.

Simon closed his eyes again, knowing what was coming. Perhaps the ground might open up just then and swallow him, he thought. Swallow all of them.

"I heard you fine," said Uncle Philbert, whom the ground refused to swallow. "I just wanted to know, how do I do *what*? Cartwheels? Algebra? The dishes? You see, there's a different answer for—"

"Maxwell," shouted Mr. Hackney, "get these people out of our way. You've got two seconds to get in this car!"

"Yes, sir!" said Simon's father, a look of numb horror on his face. Simon felt his own sense of horror melting away. He slipped his hand into his father's and looked up at him.

"Don't go," he said. "Come to my party. Please, Dad."

Mr. Maxwell looked at Simon's solemn face and then at Mr. Hackney's purple one. Then he saw Aunt Mattie, who had reappeared beside the limo window. She was carrying something under her arm.

"Why, George Maxwell," she said. "Have you forgotten everything I taught you when you were a boy?"

Simon looked from one to the other in amazement. "Taught *him*?" he asked in surprise. "Dad, did you have un-lessons, too?"

"Un-lessons?" said Mr. Maxwell slowly. "Yes, un-lessons . . ."

"Two seconds, Maxwell."

But Mr. Maxwell was looking at Aunt Mattie. Suddenly, his expression changed. He looked like someone who has finally remembered his dream of the night before. A smile crept over his face, and he looked down at Simon. "Un-lessons," he repeated.

"Well," said Hackney. "I'm waiting for an answer."

"No, no," said Mr. Maxwell distractedly, not even looking at Hackney. "No, I'm not coming."

"What? *What?* Have you lost your mind?"

"No, Mr. Hackney. I haven't lost my mind. I'm going to stay here and go to my son's birthday party. And I would like to add, sir"—here, he bent over in order to stare straight into Hackney's face, and Simon tightened his grip on his father's arm—"I would like to add that I have always felt that you, Mr. Hackney, are a bottom-feeding, talent-free, money-grubber. Sir."

Mr. Hackney gasped. "Maxwell," he hissed, "I'll give you exactly one second to apologize for that nonsense and get in this car or else—"

"Or else what?" asked Uncle Philbert. "Or else you'll give him two seconds?"

"I've got it!" said Mattie.

"What?" said the startled Hackney.

"The solution to the goldfish problem. You see, life is so boring for goldfish." She produced the fishbowl with a flourish. "But you've got this big car with a great view. All this tinted glass! And that place there"—she pointed to the liquor bar between the front and back seats—"that's a perfect spot for the bowl. I was going to give these fish to Simon for his birthday, but this is a much better home for them. Here you go. Don't bother to say thank you, really. Just remember to feed them twice a day."

Mr. Hackney's jaw dropped. Mattie thrust the bowl through the window and onto the liquor bar. The cat, Raspberry, having escaped from Mattie's car, chose that exact moment to make his move on the fish. He leaped through the open window, landing in Mr. Hackney's lap. Mr. Hackney yelped and dropped his car phone. The

phone landed in the goldfish bowl, the goldfish bowl landed—upside down—in Mr. Hackney's lap, and the fish themselves landed on the car seat.

"Maxwell!" sputtered Hackney. "This is outrageous!" He turned to the client beside him. "I'm terribly, *terribly* sorry, sir." And then to Simon's father again: "Apologize instantly or you're fired."

"I beg to differ," said Mr. Dubble Bubble, climbing out of his side of the car and handing Raspberry over to Mattie. "It is you, Mr. Hackney, who are fired. Where I come from, we treat our employees with more respect than that."

Mr. Hackney looked amazed. The color drained from his face.

"But what about Dubble Bubble gum? You can't mean this. What about our dinner?"

Simon spoke up. "I'm sure Mother can set another place for dinner. You're welcome to eat with us."

Mr. Dubble Bubble looked pleased. "I'd be honored to join your birthday party." He glanced at Hackney. "I won't be needing your services anymore, Mr. Hackney."

Mr. Hackney opened and shut his mouth a few times—something like a goldfish, thought Simon. Then he turned and ordered the limousine driver to leave.

"You are a fool, Maxwell," called Hackney.

"And you, sir," said Philbert, opening the car door, "are sitting on a goldfish." He plucked the fish and the bowl from the backseat. Hackney slammed the door, and the limo sped out the driveway.

Uncle Philbert waved good-bye to the car.

"Have a nice day," he said.

Happy Birthday

CHOCOLATE MARBLE *RED FROSTING*

The birthday party was probably the strangest one of Simon's short life.

At first, Mr. Maxwell sat in a kind of stupor while Aunt Bea asked him over and over, "Did you quit? Were you fired?" Then she would turn to Uncle Fred and whisper, "He's been fired. It's all that dreadful woman's fault."

But Mr. Maxwell just shook his head. "I don't know. Did I? Was I?"

Mr. Dubble Bubble gave a great laugh and clapped Simon's father on the back. "No, you weren't fired. Hackney didn't have the guts. Even after you called him a—what was it you called him?"

"A talent-free, bottom-feeding money-grubber," said Philbert happily.

"Ha! That's a good one. Gotta remember that one," said Mr. Dubble Bubble with great satisfaction.

"What do you mean, he didn't have the guts to fire me?" asked Mr. Maxwell, seeming to wake up.

"He didn't. He knows how good you are," said Mr. Dubble Bubble. "He showed me your ad copy—'Double, double toil and trouble.' Ha! Very clever! He didn't dare lose you. You are his best writer, Mr. Maxwell. He told me so himself. Oh, he may not have treated you that way. He was going to work you to the bone, is my guess. He must have been very sure you'd never quit."

Mr. Maxwell was silent for a long moment. "Well," he said, and a grin spread across his face, "I guess he's going to find out he was wrong."

"Good for you!" said the bubble-gum magnate. "I hope you and I—"

But Simon couldn't hear what else he said, because at that moment Aunt Mattie spoke up to point out that the idea of a *birthday party* was to open *presents*, thank you very much, and not just for grown-ups to blab on and on about *business*.

Simon made a great show of loving all his presents, when what he was really loving was that his father was here to share them with him. And Aunt Mattie and Uncle Philbert. He even smiled and thanked Aunt Bea for her present—two goldfish in a plastic bag. She seemed to have forgotten that she had given Simon goldfish for his last birthday.

"That makes six," he said, adding them to the bowl with Mattie's fish. "I promise to feed them twice a day and take them for rides in the car so they don't get bored." And he exchanged a secret wink with Aunt Mattie.

From Uncle Philbert, there was a bone-handled jack-knife with a mumblety-peg blade. Philbert had also brought a huge batch of special Seventy-Three-Alarm

Chili—"for dessert." And Mattie had brought a chocolate marble cake, with red frosting. "I thought you might need an extra," she explained to Mrs. Maxwell.

"Thank you," Simon's mother said. Her cheeks were bright pink. She glanced quickly at Fred and Bea before adding, "It's Simon's favorite, you know."

When they sat down to eat, Aunt Bea and Uncle Fred refused to touch the chili, of course. They just said, "We couldn't possibly consider eating food like that." Instead, they ate spinach pasta.

When it came Simon's turn, he said, "Thank you for making the pasta, Aunt Bea, but I think I'll try this chili." Bea and Fred exchanged a glance that said, *How rude!* But Simon pretended not to see it.

When it came time for dessert, Mrs. Maxwell brought out the carrot cake, only to be greeted with a cry from Mr. Dubble Bubble. "Carrot cake! Why eat carrot cake when you have a perfectly beautiful marble cake with red frosting?"

And because he was a guest, no one could object. So they all ate marble cake for dessert. All except Aunt Bea and Uncle Fred, who insisted that they—and Parker—eat the carrot cake.

Then Simon made a wish and blew out the candles. There was a pause. Simon looked at his father. He wanted to tell him that he'd already gotten his wish.

"Dad, I—" began Simon.

"Well, George," said Uncle Fred, clearing his throat loudly, "what are you going to do about a job now?"

"What?" said Mr. Maxwell.

"Um, Dad, could I—" said Simon.

"Simon, dear, you're interrupting," said Aunt Bea patiently. "Besides, you know you shouldn't speak before being spoken to."

Parker spoke for the first time.

"He was not interrupting," he said hotly. "*You* were."

There was a stunned silence all around.

"Perhaps now would be the time for me to give you your last present, Simon," said Aunt Mattie quickly. She rose from the table. "It's in the car. I'll just go get it."

As she left, Simon turned to his father and said, "Dad, I wanted to tell you that I was really proud of what you did today."

"Simon, how can you say that?" said Uncle Fred sternly. "Your father just lost his job."

"Yes," added Aunt Bea. "Six months from now, you may all be in the poorhouse. And all because of that woman."

"Just a moment," said Mr. Maxwell. " 'That woman' happens to be my aunt—and a very fine woman. And it wasn't her fault I lost my job. Heck, if I finally have the guts to stand up to Hackney—something I should have done years ago—I don't want to go handing the credit out to other people."

"Yeah, Dad, you were great," said Simon.

"I can't believe what I'm hearing," said Aunt Bea. "You're defending that woman? After she gets you fired? And she has clearly turned your son into a rude, selfish little beast. He used to be such a nice boy."

"See here, Bea—" began Simon's mother, and her voice had a ring of iron to it that Simon had never heard before.

But Mr. Dubble Bubble interrupted. "George is working for me," he said. "Isn't that right? That is, if you want to."

Mr. Maxwell smiled. "I think I'm going to go into business for myself. Be my own boss. And Dubble Bubble gum will be my first client."

Just then, Mattie returned to the dining room. In her arms was the cat Raspberry, who took one look at Simon and bounded straight into his lap. He put his paws on Simon's chest, stuck his nose into Simon's face, and purred loudly.

"Listen to that cat," said Philbert. "Purring like a pastry."

"Happy birthday, Simon," said Aunt Mattie. "Poor Raspberry was pining away for you. He simply *insisted* on coming to live with you."

Uncle Fred and Aunt Bea gasped at the same time.

"Oh, no. No, no, no. No, I'm afraid this won't do," said Bea. "We can't have cats in the house. Absolutely out of the question."

"Parker's allergies," explained Uncle Fred patiently.

"Not to mention the fleas and cat hair and, well, diseases and things," said Aunt Bea. "The cleaning lady—Doris—you know she'd have a conniption fit."

Mrs. Maxwell stood up. "Well, let her have a fit. There are other cleaning ladies out there. Besides, who needs a cleaning lady? I think he's a lovely cat."

"Are you saying that you're *keeping* the cat?" asked Aunt Bea, unable to believe her ears.

Mrs. Maxwell looked at Mr. Maxwell. They both looked at Simon. Simon buried his head in Raspberry's warm fur.

"Yes. We're keeping the cat."

This time, Simon broke the silence.

He burped.

It was a long, satisfying, and genuine burp—just the way Uncle Philbert had taught him. Then he jabbed himself in the forehead, jumped up, and ran around the table, poking everyone in the arm. Mattie and Philbert tried to explain the game, but suddenly Runcible let

loose a terrific imitation burp, and then Mr. Dubble Bubble burped, and then Parker did a pretend burp. Suddenly, the whole table—except, of course, Aunt Bea and Uncle Fred—was convulsed in laughter, everyone punching one another in the arm, stabbing themselves in the forehead, arguing over who did what first, gasping for breath, a parrot fluttering here, a cat leaping there.

Aunt Bea and Uncle Fred stood up and surveyed the amazing, ridiculous scene.

"Perhaps we'd better be leaving," said Uncle Fred, who could hardly be heard above the noise. Uncle Philbert and Mr. Maxwell had begun an armpit duet of "Happy Birthday."

"Yes, yes, perhaps you should," said Mrs. Maxwell, trying unsuccessfully to stop giggling. She turned to Uncle Philbert. "You must teach me how you do that."

Simon lay in bed that night thinking about the extraordinary day he'd had, from the battle with Mrs. Biggs, the fight with the bullies, and the amazing birthday party, to the departure of his relatives. He'd been surprisingly sorry to see Parker leave, and asked him where he thought they'd go.

"Well," said Parker with a sly smile, "Aunt Mattie has asked me to stay with her."

"No!" said Simon. "Your parents will never agree. I thought they said you were all going to some motel for the week."

"Yes," said Parker with an even slier smile. "But I plan to develop a wicked allergy to the motel carpet." He gave a little fake cough and rubbed his eyes till they were bright red. "Works every time."

120

Saying good-bye to Aunt Mattie and Uncle Philbert had been even odder.

Mr. Maxwell shook hands with Uncle Philbert through the car window.

"I'm going to teach Simon how to whittle with that knife," he said. "It's a great way to pass the time. And I remember this game called mumblety-something you once taught me. It's all coming back to me."

Mrs. Maxwell was saying good-bye to Aunt Mattie. "How does that go again?" she asked through the window.

"Mangy, mucculent misfit," repeated Aunt Mattie slowly.

"That's good," said Mrs. Maxwell. "I'll remember that."

Simon produced a box from under his arm and presented it to Aunt Mattie.

"It's a present for Hero," he explained.

Mattie peeked inside. It was the rest of Aunt Bea's carrot cake.

"Goodness, he'll love it!" she exclaimed. "What a thoughtful lad you are. You know, I swear that horse misses you. I tried to bring him today, but he wouldn't fit in the car."

"Maybe Simon will have a chance to visit again," said Mr. Maxwell.

"Maybe we all will," said Mrs. Maxwell. Then, remembering it was rude to invite yourself to someone else's house, she added, "If you'll have us, of course."

Mattie seemed to be considering this idea. "Do you play tennis?" she asked.

"Oh, I'm afraid not," said Mrs. Maxwell.

"Good. In that case, you're always welcome."

There was a knock on Simon's door, and his father came in and sat on the bed.

"Good-night, son."

"Good-night, Dad."

"What happened to 'Father'?"

"I just decided I like 'Dad' better. Do you mind?"

His father considered it. "I could learn to like it," he said. Then he noticed the pink detention slip on Simon's desk. "What's this?"

"I've been meaning to tell you about it, but, well, it's sort of a long story."

"Try me," said his father, with a rueful look. "As of now, I have all the time in the world."

So Simon told him the story of the run-in with Mrs. Biggs and the trip to the principal's office. "I guess you could say I got in trouble with my boss," he concluded, with a nervous glance at his father.

Mr. Maxwell gazed out the window for a long moment. He was trying to look severe.

"No more Mr. Nice Guy, huh?" he said at last.

"I guess not," said Simon.

"Well, son"—and a big grin split Mr. Maxwell's face, despite his best efforts—"I guess that makes two of us."

Simon laughed, and so did Mr. Maxwell. But then Simon stopped. He fixed his father with a stern look.

"It depends, of course," he said. "What exactly did you mean by *nice*?"

No More Nasty

Amy MacDonald

Pictures by Cat Bowman Smith

A Sunbu
Farrar St

Text copyright © 2001 by Amy MacDonald
Pictures copyright © 2001 by Cat Bowman Smith
All rights reserved
Distributed in Canada by Douglas & McIntyre Ltd.
Printed in the United States of America
First edition, 2001
Sunburst edition, 2005
10 9 8 7 6 5 4 3 2 1

www.fsgkidsbooks.com

Library of Congress Cataloging-in-Publication Data
MacDonald, Amy.
    No more nasty / by Amy MacDonald ; illustrated by Cat
Bowman Smith.
        p. cm.
    Summary: When Simon's great-aunt Matilda becomes
the substitute teacher for his unruly fifth-grade class,
her unique way of looking at things gives the students
a new perspective on learning.
        ISBN-13: 978-0-374-45511-8 (pbk.)
        ISBN-10: 0-374-45511-2 (pbk.)
        [1. Substitute teachers—Fiction. 2. Teacher-student
relationships—Fiction. 3. Schools—Fiction. 4. Great-
aunts—Fiction. 5. Humorous stories.] I. Smith, Cat
Bowman, ill. II. Title.

PZ7.M1463 Nn 2001
[Fic]—dc21

                                            00-31687

*For Jeremy, my best reader, and Alex
(he knows why)*

Biggs Bites the Dust

Where was Mrs. Biggs? Simon glanced at the clock over the door. It was the same kind of round, white clock you saw in every classroom you ever went into. It said 9:05.

No one had ever known Mrs. Biggs to be late—for class, for anything. She was the kind of person, thought Simon, who would be on time for her own execution by firing squad. And then she would give the firing squad a lecture for being thirty seconds late. Her last official act.

"Seventeen million," said Sebastian to Simon.

"Hunh?"

"Seventeen million poisonous snakes," Sebastian repeated patiently. "In the snake pit."

"Yeah," said Simon, returning to his work. He was writing, and Sebastian was illustrating, the second installment of a comic book series they called X-Boys. This issue was called "Big Bites Back," and they had just come to the part where a certain "Mrs. Big" falls into a snake pit.

"She survives, of course," said Simon, "because when the snakes bite her, *they* all die."

"Of course," said Sebastian.

"But," added Simon, "I've just figured out how she *does* die. In the next issue, 'Big Bites the Dust': execution by firing squad."

"Great idea."

"But I doubt even a firing squad—" He was interrupted when a photon missile struck him in the ear.

Simon looked around. He wasn't the only one taking advantage of Mrs. Biggs's absence.

Jimmy had stolen some paper rocket ships from Raggie's desk—Raggie himself was wandering the halls somewhere—and was launching them from Mrs. Biggs's desk. Ethan was trying to shoot them down using the latest photon missile technology (okay, paper clips launched from a rubber band).

And Mindy and Mandy and Mollie had formed a circle with their desks. Mollie was listening to music on headphones. The other two were writing a story called "The Three Little Biggs." They were reading aloud the part where an old wolf, freezing with cold and dying of hunger, knocks on the door of the first Little Bigg. He begs to be allowed in from the snowstorm. "You can't come in," says the first Little Bigg. "You spoke without raising your hand. You don't have a hall pass. Where's your permission slip? Bad wolf."

Bix was leading a hoop-shooting contest, using wadded-up pieces of paper and Mrs. Biggs's wastebasket, perched high atop two desks that he'd stacked next to the door.

Behind Bix, Mario sat with his head on his desk, fast asleep, as usual, despite the chaos.

And Julie was at the blackboard, entertaining the rest of the class with her extremely accurate imitation of their teacher. Julie was a large girl with expressive, dark eyes, and an unsettling habit of casting sidelong glances at grown-ups as if she didn't believe a word they said. She was also a deadly mimic. Arms folded on her chest, she was now addressing Moses Haskell in an

acid voice. Moses, a big, shy, dreamy boy with a stutter, had been a favorite target of Mrs. Biggs's sarcasm.

"Think hard, Moses," Julie was saying, peering at him over a pair of glasses that she'd pushed down to the tip of her nose. "Two plus two equals . . . ?"

"Uh, f-four?" said Moses, playing along.

"Light dawns over Marblehead!" said Julie, with a grand gesture. Marblehead being the name of a neighboring town, this had been one of Mrs. Biggs's favorite expressions. "Thank you, Mr. Einstein!" Julie gave him her nastiest smile and removed her glasses, just as Mrs. Biggs always did when she wanted to make a point. The kids around her burst out laughing.

At that very moment Herbert J. Bickle, their principal, opened the door and walked in. He was holding the missing Raggie firmly by the shoulder, and he had only a microsecond to take in the chaos in the classroom before one of Bix's just-launched "basketballs" bounced off his forehead and landed in the wastebasket.

"Yesss!" shouted Bix. "A three-pointer! A thirty-pointer!"

"Children!" cried Mr. Bickle, rubbing his head. "This is . . . please!"

The class suddenly seemed to realize just exactly who Mr. Bickle was. Something resembling silence fell. Students, desks, chairs, and wastebaskets slowly found their way back to their proper places.

Julie stuck up her hand. "Where is Mrs. Biggs?" she asked, without waiting to be called on. "She's late."

Mr. Bickle ignored her. He was a small, dapper man with white hair and a neat bow tie. When the class was finally silent and seated, he cleared his throat, and his face assumed a grave expression. "I have some bad . . . I'm sorry to say . . . it's very sad . . . for you," he began. Simon prepared himself for everyone's favorite guessing game: trying to figure out just what the heck the principal was trying to say. Mr. Bickle was famously unable to finish a sentence. "Mrs. Biggs won't be . . . that is, your teacher will not . . . in other words, she has decided to take early retirement."

"She quit?" asked Julie, managing to say in two small words what had taken Mr. Bickle a whole paragraph. Mr. Bickle nodded.

"Well, I wouldn't put it exactly . . . It would be more accurate to . . . um . . . Correct."

"Yesss!" shouted Jimmy and Ethan. They leaped from their seats and punched the air, while the rest of the class cheered. Even Simon leaned back in his chair and let out a huge sigh. But Mr. Bickle resumed.

"And so"—then, louder—"*and so*, for the last five weeks

of school you will have . . . of course we have had to hire . . . at least I'm hoping . . . should have been here by now—"

"A substitute?" asked Julie.

"All *right!*" whooped the class.

"Who's it gonna be? Mr. Croker?" That was Julie again. She could do a very good imitation of all the usual substitute teachers—and there had been many— but Simon especially enjoyed the way she did Mr. Croker, a man with a strong overbite and absolutely no sense of discipline. His day generally ended with more than half the students being sent to Mr. Bickle's office.

"Yeah, who?" clamored the students.

"I, well, that is," said Mr. Bickle. He looked at his watch and cleared his throat again. "Ahem. Which is to say, we've had a little trouble . . . It was very short notice to . . . None of the usual teachers could . . . But we did manage to find a . . . although she seems to be a bit late. Perhaps she got . . ."

There was a knock on the classroom door. The principal opened it and stepped outside. Simon could hear the sounds of murmured conversation. Then, strong and clear, came a voice that was strangely familiar to Simon Maxwell:

"Of course I am. I *always* try to be at least fifteen minutes late. Makes things far more interesting—don't you think?"

Then the door opened, and in walked Simon's great-aunt Matilda.

Death, Where Is Thy Sting?

Simon slid down in his chair until just his head was visible above the desktop. Aunt Matilda! This couldn't be happening to him. That could not be his great-aunt standing at the front of the classroom with Mr. Bickle. He opened his eyes and peeked over his desk. Yes, it was. It was Aunt Mattie. Aunt Mattie in her huge hat with fruit and flowers on it. Aunt Mattie in her orange flowered dress and apron.

Simon slid even lower in his chair. Maybe she won't see me, he thought. Maybe she won't recognize me.

From this position, Simon could see Aunt Mattie's feet. He noted with dismay that she had one high-top basketball sneaker, and one shiny brown lace-up boot. Straw and bits of mud clung to both feet, and from Matilda herself there wafted the unmistakable odor of horse and barn. It was an odor that under any other circumstances would have filled Simon with joy, for he recently had spent a deliriously happy two weeks at Aunt Mattie's farm, most of it in the barn or with the horses.

Mr. Bickle was still talking.

". . . so, class, will you please welcome, this is Mrs.,
um, Mrs.—"

"—Mrs. Maxwell," said Aunt Matilda helpfully.

"Yes. Mrs. . . . Now class, I want you to . . . and I'm
sure you will be on your very best . . . because if you're
not, I'll be seeing you in my office, and . . ." He came to
a halting halt, and turned to Aunt Matilda. "Mrs. Biggs
left a complete lesson plan that you . . . and detailed information about all the students who . . ." He handed
her a package. Then, having run out of things to say,
or having finished not finishing his things to say, he
wished her luck and left.

Aunt Mattie stood at the front of the room. She surveyed the class. The class surveyed her. "Well," said Matilda at last. "And how does all your corporosity seem to gashiate?"

The class looked blankly back at her. No one knew the correct response to such an odd question, except for Simon, and he wasn't about to open his mouth. In fact, no one said a thing, or even blinked, except for Simon, who slowly closed both eyes and hoped the whole thing would go away. And in a funny way, it did. For when he closed his eyes it was suddenly spring and he was back at Matilda's farm.

It had been the best two weeks of his life. Something had happened to him during that visit—what it was he couldn't say—but after he returned to Mrs. Biggs's class, he felt different. He *was* different. For the first time in his life he had gotten into trouble for talking back to a teacher. A simple thing, really. Mrs. Biggs had been in the middle of chewing Jimmy out, trying to embarrass him for getting a math problem wrong on the blackboard. Jimmy was no friend of Simon's—just the opposite, in fact—but without much thinking about what he was doing, Simon had stood up and corrected Mrs. Biggs. Jimmy, he pointed out, had gotten the answer *right*. She, Mrs. Biggs, had gotten it *wrong*. Shocked by back talk in one she had always trusted to behave perfectly, Mrs. Biggs had sent him to the principal's office for the first time in his life. He went, covered in glory and detention slips.

Despite what Jimmy and his friends thought, Simon had not really been a teacher's pet. He didn't like

Mrs. Biggs any more than the other kids did. She was downright nasty: rude, sarcastic, and happiest when humiliating the poorer students. It was just that Simon had hated the thought of getting into trouble. He'd rather have died than have to sit in the chair outside the principal's office, with everyone looking at him. He had straight A's, no detentions—and no friends.

But after that episode, Jimmy had seemed to change his mind about Simon. They hadn't become friends, but a sort of truce was established. Because Jimmy had been held back a year, and was bigger than all the other boys, they tended to do whatever he did. So life got easier for Simon. Even Julie looked at him with new respect. And Simon knew that in some strange way he owed it all to Aunt Mattie.

And now this had to happen. Simon opened his eyes again. There she stood at the front of the class, as real as porridge and twice as embarrassing.

"Well, no one's corporosity seems to be gashiating at all," said Matilda, unworried by the silent class. "And now, what should we do first?"

With a start of dismay Simon saw Ethan loading half a paper clip onto his rubber band. He gave Simon a wink and launched the photon missile at the school bell just above Mattie's head. It hit with a resounding clang.

"Goodness me!" said Aunt Mattie. "Are we under attack?"

"No," said Jimmy, standing up. "That's the recess bell."

Simon looked at his classmates. They were all playing along, putting away their books and pretending it

10

was recess. He sighed. His class had a reputation for destroying substitute teachers. They'd even made it into a sport: Sink the Sub.

Simon knew his Aunt Mattie had a will of iron—little would you guess it behind that cloud of white hair—but even Aunt Mattie couldn't withstand this class. Could she? No, they'd eat her alive. And then spit out the bones.

"Recess already?" asked Aunt Mattie. "Is that the schedule?"

Julie put up her hand.

"Generally speaking," said Julie seriously, "we have morning recess from now until 9:45. Then we have free time until lunch. After lunch we have lunch recess. And at 2:30 it's time to go home."

Matilda gave her a long look.

"Generally speaking," added Julie.

Jimmy's hand shot up.

"Except some days we have gym instead of free time," he said. "Or art."

"Yeah," added Ethan. "And except tomorrow. Tomorrow there are no classes, so you won't have to come to school at all. Mr. Bickle asked us to remind you about that. It's like a, a—"

"A no-school day?" said Matilda, helpfully.

"Yeah, that's it. A no-school day, for some reason I can't think of right now."

"Perhaps it's national Sucker the Substitute Day?" asked Matilda.

"Yeah, that's it," said Ethan. "Something like that."

11

He shrugged. "Oh, well," he said to the slumbering Mario. "It was worth a try." He poked Mario in the ribs. "Right, Mario?"

Mario jerked awake. "What?" he said. "Where?"

"Now, children," said Matilda sternly, "if you are going to try to pull the wool over my eyes, I expect you to do a lot better than that. Let's see a little creative persiflage, at least. Do I look as if I was born yesterday?"

"No, ma'am," said Julie with her most sincere expression. "You look like you were born a long, *long* time ago."

No one laughed. Instead, there was a brief, dense silence, while the class waited to see what would happen. Simon covered his eyes.

"I was," said Matilda with a smile. "And I'll thank you all to keep that in mind. Now then, as I was saying, where do we start?"

The class let out a long, disappointed sigh. Most of them, Simon realized, were not only expecting Matilda to zap Julie—they were hoping for it. Even Julie looked disappointed. At last Mario spoke.

"You have to take attendance," he said listlessly. Then yawned.

"I do? Why?" asked Matilda.

"Well . . ." Mario shifted in his seat. "I dunno. So you know who's here. And who's not. And who's late. You write it down."

"All right, then," said Matilda. Inside the package Mr. Bickle had given her was one of those black grading books. On the first page was a list of all the students in the class. But Matilda put the book down and took out

a notepad and pencil. She looked brightly about the room.

"Everyone who's here, please raise your hands." The whole class raised their hands. "Good. Everyone's here," she said, writing carefully on the pad. "Now, everyone who is *not* here, please raise your hands." No one raised a hand. "Good. No one's not here." She wrote some more notes on the pad. While she was looking down, Bix launched a last basketball at the trash can.

Matilda looked up. "Was anyone late this morning?" No one said a word. "Nobody? No one at all?"

Julie put up her hand.

"Oh, good. You were late," said Matilda. "I was beginning to give up hope." She spoke as she jotted down on her pad. "One person late."

"No," said Julie. "I wasn't late. I was going to say that *you* were late."

Simon held his breath. Julie was the class wise guy, but if she had said that to Mrs. Biggs, Mrs. Biggs would have vaporized her.

Instead, Matilda held up a finger. "Yes," she said with a smile. "Thank you. You are quite right. I had forgotten. I was more than fifteen minutes late." She noted this on the paper. Then she tore off the page, crumpled it up, and threw it in the wastebasket. A few people giggled and looked at one another.

"I believe," said Julie, "that you're supposed to take it down to the office."

"I am? Why?"

Everyone shrugged. They had no idea why it mat-

tered to anyone who was or wasn't late or here or not here. So Matilda sighed, bent over the wastebasket, plucked out the wadded-up ball, and started out the door.

"Wait!" cried Raggie. He was a skinny child, small for his age, and with a head of hair that looked as if it had never made the acquaintance of comb or brush. "You're supposed to give it to me. I'm the class monitor this week"—a complete lie, it was actually Simon's turn—"it's my job to take the attendance sheet down."

"And who might you be?"

"I'm Raggie."

"Well, thank you very much, Raggie," said Matilda, handing the crumpled sheet to him. Raggie looked at the ball of paper. Simon knew he was wondering if she really wanted him to take it to the office like that. But Matilda said nothing, so he shrugged and left the classroom.

Sebastian nudged Simon. "What do you want to bet he doesn't come back until recess?" Simon nodded. Raggie used any excuse he could find to get out of the classroom. Once he'd delivered the attendance, most likely he would spend the morning in the library or the bathroom. One time he'd even been caught in the empty science lab making rockets. The last substitute teacher hadn't noticed that Raggie never came back at all.

"Now," said Matilda, rubbing her hands together. "I would like some explanation of this behavior. Why was no one late but me?"

The students all looked at one another. Julie silently

mouthed the word *duh* to Simon. Simon ignored her. He slid a bit lower in his seat until only his eyes were showing.

"I *think* that's because we get warnings if we're late," Julie explained slowly and carefully.

"Come, come. Surely they don't punish you for a thing like being a tad late. 'Punctuality is the bugbear of small minds.' It's well known. Or is it 'Consistency is the bugbear of small minds'? Oh dear, I no longer remember."

"And if you get two warnings," continued Julie, "you get a detention." Seeing Matilda's blank look, she explained further. "Detention. You have to stay after school. If you get five detentions, you're suspended for a day."

"Well, well, well," said Matilda. "I always say, if you live long enough, you see everything." She shook her head. "From now on, things are going to be different. I have no problem with people being late. In fact I always try to be a little late myself. It makes things more interesting.

"For example, I was late getting here today because on my way I saw a poor dead porcupine by the side of the road. Now I find dead porcupines fascinating. Well, live ones are even better, aren't they, but beggars can't be choosers and besides it's *so* difficult to get really close to a live porcupine. They seem to mind if you poke your face right into theirs and ask to borrow a few quills. So this was an opportunity not to be missed. I borrowed a few of his quills—he won't need them anymore, poor thing—and then gave him a proper burial."

15

She went over to her purse—it was more like a small suitcase, actually—and pulled out a plastic sandwich bag filled with black-and-white quills. Twenty-four quills, to be precise.

"Cool!" said Ethan.

"Now," said Matilda, "that's what I did while I was being late. What did *you* do while I was being late?"

Simon stared at the ceiling. The other students looked at each other uncertainly and said nothing. Matilda picked up one of Raggie's paper rocket ships, looked at it with interest, and placed it on her desk.

"In the future," she said, "I expect more of you to be late. All you need is a perfectly good excuse, like a dead porcupine. And if I am late, I hope you will have something to show for it. Is that understood?"

The children all looked at one another and nodded dumbly.

"Something like this very fine space vehicle," she continued, "which belongs to whom?"

"It's Raggie's," said Bix.

"And speaking of Raggie," said Matilda, "where the devil has he gotten to?"

The Usual Tricks

Raggie returned much sooner than anyone expected. In fact, he was propelled back into the classroom by the school secretary, Miss Boynton, who had a firm grip on his elbow and a businesslike glint in her eye. Simon knew Miss B was not an unkind person, but she was perpetually overworked and harassed by children who had forgotten their lunches or imagined they were sick or got themselves hit by snowballs at recess, and by parents who could never remember which day was early release day or neglected to send in the proper field-trip forms or resolutely forgot to pay for their children's school lunches. Not to mention principals who never finished their sentences.

She opened the door, surveyed the class, and gave Matilda Maxwell a pitying look.

"He's up to his usual tricks," she said, pushing Raggie through the door. "He had the nerve to pretend *this* was the attendance sheet." She held out a much crinkled sheet of paper.

Mrs. Maxwell took the sheet from Miss Boynton and read aloud, " 'Ethan is a jerk. He has scummy teeth.' "

The class tittered. Bix jabbed Jimmy in the ribs and covered his mouth with his hands. Ethan glared at both of them.

"My, that doesn't sound like the attendance report."

"And he handed it to me all crumpled up in a ball," added the secretary. "I've given him a warning."

"Just a minute," said Matilda. "I think I know what happened."

She fished around in the trash can, which was full of wadded-up "basketballs" from Bix's game that morning. She pulled out another crumpled sheet of paper, unfolded it, and handed it to Miss Boynton. "There, I

gave him the wrong sheet. That's the right one. It's entirely my fault. I think there was some confusion over wastebaskets and waste-basket-balls this morning. This note"—she held up the sheet from Miss Boynton—"must belong to someone else in the class." She gazed slowly around the room and then dropped the sheet on Bix's desk. "It must belong to our basketball star. And you would be . . . ?"

"Bix." He was struggling not to laugh.

"Well, Bix, would you mind opening your mouth?"

Bix looked baffled but did as he was told. Matilda peered inside. She turned to Ethan.

"I suppose you are Ethan with the scummy teeth?" Ethan nodded. "Well, you'll be pleased to know that Bix has scummy teeth, too. I would like both of you to spend more time brushing. And it wouldn't kill you to floss, young man." This last comment was directed at Bix, who had buried his head in his arms.

"Excuse me," said Miss Boynton. She was frozen in the doorway, covered with confusion, reading the new attendance report. "This just says, 'Everyone's here. No one's not here. I was late.' "

"That's correct," said Matilda crisply. "I was late. I get a warning."

"But—"

"And Raggie doesn't. Fair's fair. Now off you go." And she hurried the harassed young woman out the door. "We have important work to do."

Funny

Matilda looked around at the class. "I suppose we better start by learning one another's names. My name is Matilda Maxwell, but everyone calls me Mattie. Except you. I'm very old, seventy-four years old, so you will have to call me Mrs. Maxwell. Unless of course"—the tiniest pause—"unless you happen to be my great-nephew or -niece, in which case you may call me Aunt Mattie." Here Simon gave a guilty start, but Aunt Mattie continued as if she hadn't noticed a thing. "I have three llamas, that's spelled with two *l*s, and goodness knows how many cats, and some peacocks, and two horses. Oh, yes, and a husband, too. His name is Mr. Maxwell."

Julie looked at Simon and once again mouthed *duh* at him. Simon gave her a weak smile. He was wondering what the chances were of someone he knew dying in the next ten minutes and his being called to the office and excused from school. For the rest of his life.

Aunt Mattie walked over to the front row. "Now let's start here. What's your name?" she asked a boy in the front row. Simon groaned inwardly. She could hardly

have picked a worse person to start with. Simon knew Jimmy would do his best to make things impossible for Aunt Mattie.

Jimmy looked Aunt Mattie straight in the eye.

"My name is Mario," he said. This drew a loud snort from Ethan and several others. Matilda smiled at Jimmy absentmindedly and then asked if she could see his hat. He looked surprised, but removed his baseball cap. She turned it over in her hands curiously.

"The Chicago Bulls," she said. "Is that a meat-packing plant?"

The class burst out laughing. Jimmy rolled his eyes at Ethan. "No," he said. "It's a basketball team. Only the most famous basketball team in the world."

"I see," said Matilda. "And this, then, must be a basketball hat?"

More laughter. Simon wished fervently for a lightning bolt to strike him dead.

"No," said Jimmy. "It's a *baseball* hat."

"I see," said Matilda. "A baseball uniform with the name of a basketball team on it. Very peculiar. But, Mario, do I look like a baseball coach?" The class laughed, and she gestured to the other students. "Does this look like a baseball game?" Several students laughed, and Bix said, "She got you there, Jimmy." Jimmy shrugged, and Matilda went and hung his cap from a coat peg. "From now on, *Jimmy*," she said, with emphasis on *Jimmy*, "I don't expect students to wear baseball caps in class, except, of course, for those times when we are actually playing baseball. Also, I expect

21

them to remember their names. Now then, do you have brothers or sisters?"

"No," said Jimmy, glowering.

"Yes, you do," said Bix, looking surprised. He turned to Matilda. "His brother is this really, really big deal on the high school basketball team. He's going to Duke on a scholarship. And his sister, Emily, she won a national piano contest or something."

"How very exciting," said Matilda. "And do you play sports, or an instrument?"

"Yeah," said Jimmy, shooting Bix a dirty look. "I'm training for the Junior Olympics. As a skeet shooter."

Matilda nodded seriously but said nothing. She then continued around the class. Mandy volunteered that she had one brother and three guinea pigs. Raggie explained that his real name was Frank but he was called Raggie.

"Don't tell me," interrupted Mrs. Maxwell. "You are called Raggie because you have the misfortune to have an older sister who couldn't pronounce your name correctly when you were born."

"Yeah," said Raggie. "How'd you know that?" Simon wished he could tell him that sometimes there were things that Aunt Mattie just *knew*. Once he had been convinced she was a witch.

"Just a good guess. It's a terrible thing to have an older sister."

Raggie nodded. "You aren't kidding," he said. "I have six of them."

When it came to Julie's turn, Simon winced. With

Julie you could never tell what would happen. Jimmy was a menace and a bully, determined to create trouble where, when—and to whom—he could. But at least he was predictable. Julie simply enjoyed being the center of attention. She usually managed to do this by making fun of the grown-ups around her—all grown-ups were fair game, it was nothing personal. (Julie was the one who had invented the game of Sink the Sub.) She had a knack for telling uncomfortable truths, which grown-ups found unnerving. It was equaled only by her talent for telling outrageous lies, which kids found entertaining.

She rose now from her seat with a solemn expression.

"My name is Julie Biedermeyer," she said. "I am the oldest of eight children. My mother"—here she swallowed painfully and looked down at the desk for a moment—"my mother died last year in a"—her voice choked briefly but she went on—"in a tragic meat-packing accident." She sat down abruptly. Beside her Mandy and Mindy were trying hard to keep a straight face.

Matilda nodded gravely. "And what would be the names and ages of your brothers and sisters?"

"Well," said Julie, caught off guard, "there's baby Joey, he's one. And, uh, the twins, two sets of twins in fact: Hughie and Louie, age two, and Harry and uh Larry, they're three. And Elsie, she's four, and Ralph, he's five, and Susie, she's eight, and uh, Sally's nine."

"Let's see, that makes ten children by my count," said Matilda. "You may not be good at math, but your skills as a thespian are impressive. Most impressive. A nice bit of cabotinage."

"Hunh?" said Julie.

"I think she means," hissed Mindy in her ear, "that you're a good actor."

Matilda circled Julie's desk, looking at her carefully. "My guess would be . . . only child."

"Hey!" cried Julie, looking around. "Someone snitched. Who told her?"

"Oh, she just knows," said Simon under his breath. Julie gave him a questioning glance, but he had sunk so low in his chair, in an effort to become invisible, that he could see nothing.

And then it was Simon's turn. There was no more avoiding it. He would not be suddenly summoned to the office. The earth would not open and swallow him. School would not be called off because of a sudden meteor shower. So he pulled himself up in his seat.

"I'm Simon Maxwell," he said, speaking loudly. "I have no brothers or sisters. I have some goldfish, though. And . . . and a pet cat named Raspberry. Which my great-aunt gave me." He looked Aunt Mattie in the eye. Now it would happen. Now everyone would discover that this Mrs. Maxwell was his great-aunt. He wondered if anyone had ever actually died of embarrassment. Actually died and been buried and had it on their gravestone: HERE LIES SIMON. DIED OF MORTIFICATION.

But Mattie gave no sign of recognizing him beyond raising her eyebrows.

"Maxwell?" she asked. "Two Maxwells in the same

room. What a funny coincidence. I'll bet we're related somehow."

"Sure," said Simon as he stared down at his desk, his cheeks burning. "That would be really funny."

Traitor

"Funny," said Aunt Mattie, after consulting her little black teacher's book, "it doesn't say anything here about free time or recess." She looked at Julie. "It says here that Monday mornings we do vocabulary." Julie batted her eyes and smiled innocently.

The class let out a collective sigh. Then they began noisily raising their desk lids and pulling out battered workbooks and pencils. Seeing Mattie's confusion, Mollie got up and found the teacher's copy of the workbook on her desk for her. She opened to Lesson 19: Parts of the Body.

"'Define the following ten words,'" Mattie read aloud, "'and use each in a sentence: *pancreas, gall bladder, trachea, kidney, femur, tibia, cranium, spleen, clavicle, appendix.*' Oh my, no. This will never do."

The children, who were already fighting over the dictionaries, for none of them had ever heard of any of the words, stopped and looked at Matilda. She was frowning at the vocabulary book, flipping through the pages. Then she tossed the whole thing into the wastebasket.

"Why'd you do that?" asked Mindy. "We always use this workbook."

"I never saw so many useless words in my life!" said Matilda. "*Pancreas!* Pah! Whoever heard of a pancreas? When would you ever need to use the word *pancreas*? Never! If your pancreas was ailing, you would go to a doctor and say, 'My belly hurts.' And the doctor would say, 'No, that's your pancreas that hurts.' And you would say, 'Thanks so much for clearing that up.' *Pancreas!* Pah!"

And she marched up and down by the blackboard, her eyes fairly snapping. Finally she stopped.

"Take out your pencils," she commanded. "Write this down." She wrote a long string of words on the blackboard:

quisling
pecksniffian
miscreant
muculent
rodomontade
proficuous
persiflage
cabotinage
sabotage
badinage
nefarious
whiffet

"Those," she said, "now *those* are useful words." She pointed to one at random. "How many people know the meaning of *quisling*? How about *proficuous*?" No one

27

raised a hand. "Very good. We'll start with *quisling*. Write down a definition for it. No, don't touch the dictionaries." The students looked blankly at her.

"But we don't know what it means," said Jimmy.

When Matilda turned away he twirled his finger by his head to indicate that Matilda was missing some of her marbles. Ethan snickered.

"Of course you don't. But you should. It's a very good word. So make up a definition that sounds like what you think *quisling* might mean. Make it sound as much like a dictionary definition as you can. Then use it in a sentence. The point is to see how many people you can fool."

Slowly the students got the idea. They sat giggling, scribbling, and staring off into space. While they worked, Matilda got a battered red dictionary out of

her carpetbag, looked up the definition of *quisling*, and wrote it on a piece of paper. Then she collected all the students' "definitions."

"Now," she said, "I'm going to read the fake definitions, as well as the real definition, and your job is to guess which is the real definition. The person who gets the most votes for his or her fake definition is the winner."

She proceeded to read out the answers. Some were stupid, but some were pretty good, Simon thought.

" '*Quisling:* noun. A short quiz. Example: The teacher gave the class a vocabulary quisling.' " Six people voted for that one.

" '*Quisling.* From the verb *to quisle*, meaning to *quickly whistle*. Example: "Could you stop that quisling?" yelled his father. "It's driving me crazy!" ' " Four people voted for that one.

Simon won the game with his: " '*Quisling:* noun. A young bird, the offspring of a *quisse*. Example: The mother *quisse* crossed the road, followed by her six little quislings.' " Eleven people voted for that one.

Nobody voted for the real definition: " '*Quisling:* noun. From the Norwegian politician Vidkun Quisling. A traitor. Example: The quisling was executed for betraying his country.' "

The Way We've Always Done It

The bell sounded, startling Aunt Mattie so much that her pencil flew straight up into the air and impaled itself in her hair. The children stuffed their papers into their desks and jumped up, heading for the door.

"What is it? What's happening?" asked Matilda.

The class ignored her and streamed out of the room. Miss Boynton poked her head inside the door.

"Is there a fire?" Matilda asked her. "A nuclear war? Don't panic, children. Everyone under your desks. Stop, look, and listen. I mean, stop, rock, and roll. That is, stop, drop, and—"

Miss Boynton gave her a strange look. "It's recess time," she explained over the hullabaloo. "You can come to the Teachers Room."

"Goodness," said Matilda. "I'm so relieved. But don't I get to go outside, too?"

Miss Boynton laughed. "No. Lucky you, you don't have recess duty this week. You can come and meet the other teachers. Who's the class monitor? Simon, would you please show Mrs. Maxwell to the Teachers Room?" And before Simon could object, she was gone.

Fortunately, the walk to the Teachers Room was short, and the corridor was so full of noisy kids that speech was impossible. Simon guided Matilda to the nurse's office and pointed to a small room, full of teachers, that opened off it.

"This is it, Aunt—I mean, Mrs. Maxwell," he said, blushing a bright red.

Aunt Mattie looked at him with an absentminded smile. "Yes," she said kindly. "Yes, you'd better call me Mrs. Maxwell when we're in school, don't you think? Thank you, dear." And she entered the room.

Simon, though he knew it was bad manners to eavesdrop, was frozen outside the door in fascination, the kind of fascination that makes you watch terrible things, like car accidents or scary movies, even though you don't want to. He simply couldn't imagine Aunt Matilda in the Teachers Room. He lingered outside the door, pretending to get a drink of water.

Matilda surveyed the Teachers Room and spoke brightly.

"Good morning, everyone. I'm Mrs. Maxwell. I've taken Mrs. Biggs's class for the rest of the year."

There was a pause in the conversation. The teachers looked up at Mattie, some of them shaking their heads and making small clucking sounds of sympathy.

"You poor dear," said Miss Frescobaldi, a small, red-headed woman who taught one of the other fifth grades. She patted Matilda on the arm. "Lucky for you there's only five more weeks of school. Hang in there, and if you need help, I'm just next door. Pound on the wall and I'll be there. That's what poor old Croker used

31

to do. How many did you send to the principal this morning?"

"Why, just Raggie, I suppose," said a surprised Matilda. "Was I supposed to send more? It seemed to me that one person was more than enough to carry the attendance sheet."

The group laughed as if Matilda had made a fine joke.

"No, dear, we mean for disciplinary purposes. When they *misbehave*," explained Miss Frescobaldi.

"But how does that discipline them?"

"It doesn't," said Mr. Farley, the other fifth-grade teacher. Charley Farley. He had sleek dark hair and reminded Simon of a seal. "But it makes them the principal's problem, not yours."

"What does he do to them?"

"He makes them sit in a chair in the hallway."

"And if they're really bad," said someone Simon couldn't see, "he sends them home."

"Which makes them the parents' problem, not the principal's?" guessed Mattie.

"Right!"

Mattie appeared to ponder this for a moment. "Let me see if I have this straight. If a child is refusing to do her multiplication tables, she is excused from math and gets to sit in a chair instead, which must be ever so much nicer than doing math. And if a child is miserable at school and refuses to behave he is given a day off and sent home to play. I'm sure there is logic in there somewhere, but I'm blessed if I can see it."

Simon covered his mouth to smother a laugh. He could see the teachers smiling and looking at one another nervously.

"Ha, ha," said one. "Now you put it like that, it seems a little odd. But it's the way we've always done it." The rest of them nodded.

There was a brief silence. Then Mr. Farley spoke up.

"How is your project coming for the County Science Fair?"

"Science Fair? Oh my. What is that?"

"Every fifth-grade class has to submit a science proj-

ect," said Mr. Farley. He had a knowing expression on his face. "It's quite a big deal. The winning entry gets a lot of prizes for the school and goes on to the State Science Fair."

"Yeah, listen to him talk," said Miss Frescobaldi. "Farley here has won the County Science Fair the last four years running, and the State Fair twice. What's your secret, Farley? How do you get all the geniuses in your class?"

Mr. Farley looked smug. "Oh, I guess it's just a case of being a good science teacher, a natural talent you might say." Simon nearly laughed out loud again. Right, he thought, a natural talent for cheating.

Mr. Farley looked around at the other two fifth-grade teachers—Aunt Mattie and Miss Frescobaldi. "Besides, it's well known that girls—oh, excuse me, I mean *ladies*—don't understand science." He laughed loudly— a short, barking sound. Just like a seal, thought Simon.

Miss Frescobaldi threw a piece of chalk at Mr. Farley. A sixth-grade teacher snorted in disgust. But Aunt Mattie just smiled. And so did Simon as he walked out to recess. He knew it never paid to underestimate his aunt Matilda.

Fruitcake for Lunch

There was only one topic of conversation at lunch that day: the new sub.

"What a wacko," said Jimmy to Simon, shoveling his limp green beans onto Simon's tray and grabbing Simon's chocolate milk in exchange.

"Trade you this sandwich for your chips, Simon?" said Mario. "Yeah, she must have escaped from the funny farm."

"Well, she definitely came off *some* kind of farm," said Julie, wrinkling her nose and waving her hands in front of it. This got a big laugh from her friends.

"Did you see her *shoes*?" said Mandy. "They don't even match!"

"No kidding," chimed in Mindy. "And that hat! It's like a fruit salad."

"Or Chiquita Banana."

Julie opened a napkin, put it on her head, and put her banana on top of that. She stood up and folded her arms like Chiquita Banana. "I am Chiquita Banana and I'm here to say," she sang in a loud voice that was a

perfect imitation of Aunt Mattie's, "how does your *por-porosity gushiate* today?"

Everyone laughed except Raggie and Simon. Raggie just grinned his crooked grin. Simon was wishing for once that no one had sat beside him at lunch. He looked around. It was too late to move to another table.

"I give her a week, max," Julie continued. "I'll bet my best pen. She's out of here in five days." She laid it on the table. It could write in four different colors. "Any takers?" Betting on how long the new teacher lasted was an important part of Sink the Sub. Jimmy put some trading cards on the table.

"Two weeks," he said.

"What?" yelped Julie. "No one's ever lasted more than a week with us. Seven days, max."

Ethan gave a shrug and looked around. "I dunno, Julie," he said. "She could be tough. She's got *you* fig-

ured out." He put a yo-yo on the table. "I'm with Jimmy. Two weeks."

"Are you nuts?" cried Julie. "She's a fruitcake! And we're the worst class in the school." Julie's followers looked at Julie. Jimmy's followers looked at Jimmy. Mindy put her new eraser on the table. "I know she's a fruitcake," she said, "but Ethan's right. Two weeks. Sorry, Julie." And one by one everyone else followed suit.

"What about you, Simon?" asked Julie suddenly. "You're being real quiet. Wait a minute—don't tell me you *like* that freak!"

"Omigod, he's gonna be Mrs. Maxwell's little goody-goody," said Jimmy with a sneer. "Just like with Mrs. Biggs. I should've known it wouldn't last."

Simon felt desperate. All eyes were on him. Aunt Mattie just happened to be his favorite relative in the world. Why couldn't he acknowledge her, just tell everyone she was his great-aunt and tell them to shut up about it? What was it about seeing her in front of all his classmates that was so embarrassing? Why was he having to choose between his aunt and his newfound friends?

"She's not so bad," said Simon at last. "She kept Raggie from getting a warning."

A groan of disgust went around the table. Jimmy picked up his tray and moved to a different seat. Before he left, he grabbed Simon's brownie and stuffed it into his ravioli. "Teacher's pet," he hissed.

Simon took a deep breath—he was going to say more, he was going to tell them she was his great-aunt

and tell them to shut up about it, he was—but just then Sebastian delivered a sharp kick to his shins. Simon saw that everyone sitting opposite him was looking frozen. He turned around to see what they were all staring at.

Aunt Mattie, lunch bag in hand, was standing right behind him. How long had she been there? How much had she heard? "Is there room for one more?" she asked cheerfully. There was a shocked silence.

"Teachers," said Julie in her direct way, "always eat in the Teachers Room. Unless they have cafeteria duty."

"Oh my," said Aunt Mattie. "So many rules." And she sat down anyway, in the spot Jimmy had vacated. She unrolled the top of her lunch bag, oblivious to the silence at the table, oblivious also to the bread roll, launched from a different table, that hit Moses on the forehead and landed in his ravioli. Moses picked it up and munched it absentmindedly.

"You want to have lunch with *us*?" asked Mario.

"Yes," said Matilda primly. "The Teachers Room is so dreary. And they don't have chocolate milk." She pulled an enormous slab of cake out of her lunch bag. "Questions?"

Silence.

"No questions? Didn't anyone ever teach you to ask questions?"

"Not at school," said Mindy.

"Well, then why are you at school?"

"To learn stuff, I guess."

"And how do you imagine you learn stuff without asking questions?"

"You write down what the teacher says. *She*'s the one who asks the questions. Like on tests," offered Julie in a slow, I'm-speaking-to-an-idiot-here voice. "We get to *answer* the questions."

"Well, I was always told that the only way to learn something was by *asking* questions," said Aunt Mattie, munching on cake. "And people who don't ask questions are very boring. Like furniture—right, Simon? Furniture doesn't ask questions, and it's dreadfully boring to have around. (My goodness, do you always eat ravioli on your brownie?) So I say again: Questions?"

Julie got that smirk on her face that always preceded some wisecrack.

"Okay," she said, putting down her sandwich. "Why is the sky blue?"

"I don't know," said Matilda. "Because it is. Next question?"

"How many stars are there in the sky?"

"Exactly enough. Enough to read by in some parts of the world. Enough to make you feel really small and unimportant. Next?"

"Have you ever taught before?"

"For one year. When I was twenty."

"Aren't you too old to be a teacher now?"

Matilda, having finished the cake, took a large cucumber sandwich from her bag and began eating that.

"Sometimes," she said, "doing things backward seems to make so much more sense."

"Yeah," muttered Sebastian to Simon, "like eating your dessert first."

"For example, some people take up teaching and

then retire. Like Mrs. Biggs. I retired and then took up teaching.

"Perhaps a better question would have been: Wasn't I too young to teach when I was twenty? Why, when I was twenty, what did I know? Precious little, I can promise you that. Did I know how to change the spark plugs on a V-8 engine? I did not. Did I know what peacock eggs taste like? What a mackerel sky or a red sunset means? How to remove porcupine quills from a dog's nose? That people blink their eyes when they're lying or nervous? How many stars there are in the sky?" She shook her head sadly.

"You still don't know that," Mario pointed out.

"Yes, but I know now that it doesn't matter. In fact, I never want to know exactly how many stars there are. Some things it's best to leave undiscovered. It inspires the imagination. More questions?"

"Why do you wear different shoes?"

Aunt Mattie looked at her feet, as if seeing them for the first time. "Because don't you just love new shoes?" she said. "And hate them, too—they make your feet hurt so. Having two feet hurting all day is a misery, so I break in new shoes one at a time."

"And tomorrow you'll wear the other two?"

"That's right."

Julie rolled her eyes. Everyone else snickered. Simon looked long and hard at his ravioli. He counted them. Thirteen. He had thirteen raviolis. Would lunch never end? Would this day never end?

Stop That Quisling!

Julie lived near Simon's street, and just recently (on those days when Simon didn't take the bus) she had taken to walking home with him. She hadn't asked him. She'd just appeared, sometimes bringing a crowd of giggling girls with her. Simon, who was shy in big groups, pretended to find this tiresome and often ignored them. Secretly, though, he had to admit he found the attention somewhat interesting and even a bit flattering. Today, however, Julie was by herself. Being Julie, she didn't say Hello, or Hey, or any kind of introductory remarks. She just said, "I can't be*lieve* you like that nutcase."

"Well," said Simon, "I—"

"She's a real space cadet, that's what she is. Boy, those shoes! And what about the way she . . ."

Simon slowly tuned out what Julie was saying. One thing about Julie was that she loved the sound of her own voice. Usually this got on Simon's nerves, but today he discovered that it had its good side. It meant he didn't have to do any talking. In a funny way it was kind of peaceful. He could think about whatever he

liked, if only he remembered from time to time to say Yeah, or Really? to make it seem like he was listening. And right now he needed to think about what to do about Aunt Mattie.

Aunt Mattie. In a weird way, what had just happened to him was funny. (His dad would have used the word *ironic*.) Simon liked to think that he had had some small part in ridding the school of Mrs. Biggs. That day two months ago, when he had talked back to her for the first time, something in Mrs. Biggs had seemed to snap. She got crabbier and crabbier. And now this—early retirement. Yet Simon also knew that all this change—the change in him, the change in the attitude of the other kids, perhaps even the disappearance of Mrs. Biggs— was due in some strange way to Aunt Mattie, to the two weeks he had spent on her farm.

So Mattie had gotten rid of Mrs. Biggs and helped him make his first friends. And now here she was taking Mrs. Biggs's place and threatening to destroy his budding friendships. Talk about irony!

Okay, the solution was easy. He would just tell everyone she was his great-aunt. What was so hard about that? Well, for one thing, Simon answered his own question, it's way too late. What am I supposed to do, say, Oh, I've just remembered, she's my great-aunt? That would be twice as embarrassing.

"What would?" asked Julie.

"Huh?"

Julie looked pained. "You're talking to yourself. You haven't heard a word I've been saying, have you?"

"Not really." He paused, then turned to Julie. "Can I

ask you a question? Do you ever notice that stuff that seems okay at home seems really dumb at school?"

"What do you mean? Like the food your mother makes? Your lunches and stuff?"

"Yeah. Exactly."

"Tomato sandwiches seem completely normal at home, in fact they taste really good. But when you bring them to school, everybody is like, Gross! And you look at them and they suddenly *do* seem gross. But you never noticed it when your mother makes them for you at home. Stuff like that?"

"That's just what I mean," said Simon, amazed that anyone else might know about this.

"Sure," said Julie. "It's well known. It's the Parallel Universe Phenomenon. School and home exist in two parallel, never-overlapping universes. If by chance they do overlap, disaster."

It made sense. Two separate and distinct universes in a kid's life: There was home, and then there was school. Things that are normal at home are hideous at school. Take his mother's winter coat, for example, or her shoes. Simon hardly noticed and rarely cared what his mother wore around the house. When she showed up at school, however, on those blessedly few occasions, he became painfully aware that her shoes were old-fashioned, that her winter coat was frumpy—no, *ridiculous* was not too strong a word for it. His father, who was a nice enough guy at home, became Super Nerd when he walked through the school door. Why did he wear those really stupid cardigan sweaters? Good grief—*nobody* wore button-up sweaters! Nobody but Mr. Rogers from the kiddie TV show. Did his dad live in a different time zone? A different universe? Yes, a different universe. That was the answer.

And so it had been with Aunt Mattie. That hat! That dress! When he'd been on Mattie's farm, sure they looked a little different, but different had seemed fine, even wonderful. But that was home. This was school. Under the fluorescent glare of the school lights and the disbelieving stares of the other students, Aunt Mattie suddenly seemed like something from a circus.

"So when, say, your parents come to school, do you wish they wouldn't?"

"Of course," said Julie.

"You don't think that's like . . . betraying them?"

"No way! I mean, why should I have to suffer just because my mother decides to drive the world's dorkiest car? Or because my father wears rubbers over his shoes?"

Simon couldn't believe someone else knew about these things. Julie was smart. You could tell by the way she understood stuff that no one else did. She might even understand about Aunt Mattie. He turned to her.

"Julie—" he began, but Julie was still talking, and you might as well try to stop a freight train as stop Julie when she was still talking.

"Sometimes," she was saying, "sometimes I pretend I don't know them. Sometimes I even wish my parents had a different last name so no one would know we are related, you know what I mean?"

"Yeah," said Simon. "It's funny you said that because—" But Julie was still talking.

"Hey, and speaking of having the same last names, you and Mrs. Maxwell—"

This time it was Julie who was interrupted as Mindy, Mandy, and Sebastian overtook them on the sidewalk. "Still talking about the sub?" Sebastian asked Julie. They ignored Simon.

Instead of answering, Julie pulled off her glasses and put them on top of her head, as Aunt Mattie frequently did. "Goodness me," said Julie in her best Aunt Mattie voice, groping blindly around. "Where are my blessed glasses? Who are you? Where am I?"

Sebastian laughed. He, Mindy, and Mandy walked off with Julie, giggling loudly as they went. Simon watched

them go. Julie had apparently forgotten he was in the middle of talking to her.

"Look!" cried Mindy. She wore her hair in a ponytail, and this allowed her to take two pencils and stick them into her hair, exactly as Aunt Mattie had stuck pencils into the hair she wore at the back of her head in a loose bun. "I know I have a pencil somewhere," said Mindy, looking vaguely around. This brought fresh gales of laughter from everyone. Simon couldn't stand it anymore.

"Stop!" he said. Everyone turned to stare at him.

"Stop what?" said Julie.

Simon hesitated, feeling all eyes on him. "Stop, rock, and roll!" It was his best imitation of Aunt Mattie's voice. "Don't panic, children. Is it a nuclear war?"

Sebastian laughed. Julie laughed. The whole group laughed. Simon laughed until his sides hurt.

No, she was no relative of his. The names? Just a coincidence. There were plenty of Maxwells in the world. Betrayal? Simon would have denied her three— no, thirty—more times before the day was done.

Please and Thank You

The bell rang at precisely twenty-three minutes past eight the next morning. Simon was already at his desk. Students poured into the classroom, shouting and jostling each other. At precisely twenty-seven minutes past eight, Aunt Mattie appeared in the doorway, completely out of breath and with her hair in wild disarray. In one hand she carried her suitcase of a purse, in the other a large covered cage. Simon recognized that cage, and he smiled in spite of himself.

Aunt Mattie glanced up at the clock.

"Oh dear. Only four minutes late. I must remember to wear my watch tomorrow, so I can be a little less punctual."

She placed the cage in the well under her desk, removed her coat, and began trying—with absolutely no success at all—to pin her hair back up on top of her head.

"Well, and how does your corporosity seem to gashiate this morning, children?" she puffed. She looked about the room expectantly, but again nobody seemed to have the foggiest idea how to answer this

question. Simon alone knew that the correct response was "very discombobulate, great congruity, dissimilarity" (whatever that meant). But he bowed his head and kept silent.

Aunt Mattie beamed at the class nonetheless. "Let's see," she said. "If I'm correct, the first thing to do today is to take attendance. Everyone who's here, raise your hands, please. Hmm. Everyone's here. Now everyone who's not here, please raise your hands. Hmmph. It would appear that no one's *not* here." She noted this down and then glared around the room. "Did I not tell you quite clearly yesterday that I expect you to be a little late at least some of the time? Well? Yes, Julie."

"Excuse me, Mrs. Maxwell, ma'am," she said, standing up with a fake-serious expression on her round face. "But Bix isn't here." She pointed to his empty seat and sat down with a sly smile.

"Well," said Matilda crisply, "why didn't he raise his hand then? Hmm?" She bent over her desk and noted Bix's absence on a piece of paper. While doing this, and without raising her eyes from the desk, she said, "And Simon, would you like to share that note with the whole class, please."

Simon, caught dead in the act of passing a note from Julie to Mindy, glanced at the piece of paper, saw what Julie had written about Aunt Mattie, and blushed deep red. "I, um—" he stammered. Simon's cheeks were so hot he thought they might actually burst into flame. Julie, seeing that he was about to read the note, shot him a dirty look and snatched the paper from his hand. She glanced at the note.

"It says, 'I think Mrs. Maxwell is the most excellent teacher in the whole world, don't you agree?'" And before anyone could move, she crumpled up the note into a little ball, put it in her mouth, chewed twice, and swallowed it. Mrs. Maxwell waited for the laughter to die down.

"Thank you, my dear," she said. "Well, I've heard of people having to *eat their words* before, but this is the first time I've actually seen it done in public."

The class laughed again, even louder, and Simon breathed a sigh of relief. He would have to say that that round went to Aunt Mattie (and Julie, looking sulky, clearly knew it). But he was mainly relieved to have been saved from reading the note aloud.

"Now then, class," began Aunt Mattie, "where were we? Oh, yes. Attendance. Well, we've finished with that." She tossed the sheet aside. "Let's get down to the business of learning something. Today we do science." She marched to the front of the class. "In science today we are going to study the feather and the quill—"

At that moment, the teacher's desk, which had never been known to speak before, said:

"Shut up!"

The students sat in stunned silence. Not only had the desk spoken for the first time in memory, but it had used a loud, raspy, and disrespectful voice. A voice that Simon knew only too well.

"Oh dear," said Aunt Mattie, bending down and peering under her desk. "Now, Runcible, if you wish to come to school, I expect you to set a better example for the children. At the very least, you must learn to say *please:* 'Shut up, *please.*' Do you hear me?"

49

She pulled the large cage out from its hiding spot, placed it on the desk, and removed the cover. Inside was a big gray parrot, preening her feathers in a way that could only be described as self-satisfied. She gave Mattie a steely look.

"Say please," said the parrot, cocking her head. "Say thank you." And then, in rapid fire like a machine gun, "Pleasethankyoupleasepleasethankyoupleasethankyouthank—"

"Oh, do shut up!" said Mattie irritably, placing the cover back on her cage.

"Say please!" added Runcible in a muffled voice.

"Please," said Matilda meekly, looking embarrassed. "She always has to have the last word. Such a badly behaved creature."

At this point the class could no longer contain its glee.

"It's a parrot!" they shouted.

"No, it's not," said Matilda. "It's a science experi-

ment." And she removed a feather from the bottom of Runcible's cage and put the cage back under her desk. "A very badly behaved science experiment. As I was saying, the quill—"

Matilda was startled by a loud bell a few feet from her desk. The feather flew into the air. Matilda gave the bell a fierce look and waited impatiently for it to finish jangling.

"Not a nuclear war?" she asked the class.

"No," said Julie. "Just the first bell."

Matilda retrieved the feather and continued: "As I was saying, we are going to study the feather and the quill." From one of the many pockets in her apron she produced the porcupine quills. From another she produced a giant magnifying glass.

"The quill—" Here she was interrupted yet again, this time by Mandy.

"Is this for Science Fair?" she asked. "Because—"

"No," said Matilda tartly. "This is because I found a porcupine yesterday. Now then, the quill—" Overhead, the PA system gave off a loud crackle.

"Good morning, children," came a raspy voice from

the PA, sounding remarkably like Runcible. "Time for morning announcements." The voice began to drone on and on. Morning announcements appeared to be the signal for everyone in the class to start talking at once. Sebastian elbowed Simon. Mandy passed a note to Mindy. Jimmy tried to pull another boy's chair out from under him. And Raggie and Julie announced that they needed to go to the bathroom—*please,* said Julie, she couldn't hold it any longer *please* could she have a bathroom pass please please *please.*

Mrs. Maxwell simply stood at the front of the class, still holding the quill, feather, and magnifying glass, but with an expression on her face that did not bode well. Simon knew that look. It was the look that Uncle Philbert, Aunt Mattie's husband, often got when he was about to let someone have it. But he'd seen it on Aunt Mattie's face only once, when she chewed out a young policeman for speeding.

Gradually the class settled down. Julie decided that she really could hold it. Raggie, nailed by a look from Aunt Mattie, stopped trying to sneak out the door. And Sebastian told Simon to shut up *please.*

Matilda drew a long breath and began a fifth time. "The quill—"

This time the door opened, and the assistant principal stuck his head in the room.

"Attendance sheet!" he announced importantly. "We don't have your attendance sheet, Mrs. Maxwell."

Aunt Mattie turned to face him.

Simon closed his eyes and prayed for a miracle. This was not going to be pretty.

52

5-3, Aunt Mattie

The assistant principal's name—to the delight of the students—was Otis Lister. Mister Lister. He had a long, thin face and long, thin hair combed back over his balding head. His eyes bulged slightly, which Simon thought made him look like a fish, and his face wore a perpetually pinched and put-upon look. It was the look of someone who had spent his entire childhood putting up with a great deal of teasing about his first name. It was the look of someone who had spent his entire adult life putting up with a great deal of impertinence about his last name. It was the look of an assistant principal who spent most of his day dealing with paperwork. An assistant principal who thought he should have been made head principal long, long ago.

"Your attendance sheet is late," repeated Mr. Lister. "I hope—"

"Mr. Lister," interrupted Aunt Mattie tartly, "did no one ever teach you it is bad manners to interrupt?"

Mr. Lister's face went blank.

"I beg your—"

"Interrupting! It's very rude. And was that you on the public address system this morning?"

"Well, yes, I always—"

"So that makes twice you have interrupted my class. And the bell makes three."

That was not entirely fair, as it wasn't Mr. Lister's fault that the bells went off when they did. Nonetheless, Simon began to enjoy this. He knew from personal experience that Aunt Mattie was a champion interrupter herself. Why, if there had been an Olympic event in Interruption, she would have been the odds-on favorite for a gold medal. Mr. Lister may have interrupted her twice this morning, but by Simon's count Aunt Mattie had already interrupted Mr. Lister three times in less than thirty seconds. It was going to be a good contest.

Simon's class, reputed to be the noisiest one in the entire history of the whole elementary school, was utterly silent. You could, thought Simon, have heard a fly sneeze.

Mr. Lister seemed frozen in time and space. Aunt Mattie, on the other hand, marched over to her desk, shuffled through an enormous heap of loose papers, found the attendance sheet at last, handed it to him, and turned back to her students.

"Now class," she began again, "the quill—"

But Mr. Lister was not going to go down in defeat quietly. He looked at the attendance sheet. Would he attempt another interruption, Simon wondered? Yes! He opened his mouth—he was going for it!

"This just says—" began Mr. Lister.

"I've given you fair warning, Mr. Lister," said Aunt

Mattie. "Which you chose to ignore. Now I'm going to have to give you a real warning." She made a note on a scrap of pink paper and then marched over to the door.

"But—"

"And if you persist," said Aunt Mattie, trying gently but firmly to close the door on him, "I'll have to send you to the principal's office. Good day, Mr. Lister."

"But—"

"Shut up!" squawked a voice from the teacher's desk. Mr. Lister poked his head back through the door. His eyes darted around the classroom in disbelief. His mouth opened and closed noiselessly, like one of Simon's goldfish. Then Aunt Mattie closed the door on him with a click. "Good riddance," the desk called out after him. And then, as if remembering a distant lesson, it added in a sulky tone, "Please."

"Really, Runcible, do you *always* have to have the last word?" asked Aunt Mattie.

"Go, Runcible!" shouted Sebastian, and everyone cheered.

"Thank you," said Runcible.

Simon added up the score on his fingers: 5–3, a clear victory for Aunt Mattie. And not just over Mr. Lister, either, he thought, looking around the class.

A Change of Plans

Aunt Mattie stood at the front of the class. She opened her mouth.

"Now, children," she began, "the quill—" But once again, before she could get any further, the bell went off. Matilda closed her mouth grimly.

"I forbid you to move," she said to the students. When the bell had finished its ringing, she placed the quill and magnifying glass back in her bag and rummaged around in it for a moment. Then she straightened up and surveyed the silent classroom.

"I've changed my mind about the science lesson today," she said. "We're not going to study quills." She glanced at the PA loudspeaker and the bell located over the door of the room. "We're going to study electricity." She held up a screwdriver and some pliers. "Does anyone have any wire cutters?"

In Which Mr. Bickle . . .

DETENTION: Otis Lister
DATE:
REASON:
SIGNED BY:

"Rank insubordination!" fumed Mr. Lister, pacing up and down. "That's what it is. Rudeness and insubordination! Why, she threatened to send me to the principal's office! Me! The assistant principal! And then she told me to shut up! She has to go. Now. I insist."

Herbert J. Bickle shifted in his chair. He squared the edges of some papers on his desk. He cleared his throat. "I see. Yes. Clearly she has behaved in a fashion that is most, and that we . . . understand your . . . However, the fact remains that we cannot, we simply *cannot* afford . . . Otis, you have no idea how many substitutes we called before we found Mrs., uh . . . But at such short notice we couldn't, we just . . . and furthermore the class has a reputation for devouring substitute teachers, quite shocking and, that is to say, and those few people who *could* come at short notice didn't *want* to tackle such a challenging group of, of—"

"Of smart alecks and dunces," said the exasperated Mr. Lister, finishing at least one sentence for Mr. Bickle.

"Well, I would not choose . . . Those exact words are

not how I myself would describe . . . Granted they are a challenging—"

"So we're stuck with this Maxwell woman, is that what you're telling me?"

"In a word, um."

Mr. Lister turned away to hide his irritation. Then he had a sudden inspiration. "Why don't you let me take over the class? I could whip those kids into shape in no time."

Mr. Bickle looked astonished. "You? Take over the . . . ? But I thought you hated the kids in that . . . and teaching is not your, not your best . . . "

"I'm a great teacher," said Mr. Lister. "The students all love me. They do. Children always appreciate firmness and discipline."

"Otis. It won't, it's not . . . I hate to disappoint . . . "

But Mr. Lister stormed out before Mr. Bickle could finish not finishing his sentences, leaving Mr. Bickle staring at the empty space in front of his desk where Otis Lister had so recently been.

For Richard Stands

"There," said Aunt Mattie with a sigh. "Perhaps now we'll have some peace and quiet."

Simon climbed down off the chair, and the class stared at the disassembled PA system and bell. Wires stuck out of the wall in every direction. Several students giggled.

His great-aunt walked to the blackboard and began drawing a diagram of wires and batteries, talking as she went.

". . . and so," she concluded, "it is perfectly clear, is it not, how electricity works?" The sound of a bell ringing could be heard in Miss Frescobaldi's classroom next door. "Can anyone explain why our bell is not ringing at this moment? Mollie?"

But Julie stuck her hand up first.

"Yes, Julie? Can you explain to us why the bell is not ringing?"

"Well, I was going to say, are we still doing Science? Because Science goes from 8:43 until 9:15. It's 9:15 now. Time for Social Studies. That goes until 9:48."

Matilda looked amazed. "Do you mean to tell me you

have thirty-two minutes for Science, then you stop whatever you're doing and do Social Studies for thirty-three minutes?"

The class all nodded.

"Why?" asked Aunt Mattie.

"I don't know," said Julie. "That's just the way it's always done."

"Perhaps, " said Matilda, pacing in front of the blackboard, "perhaps they think because you are young whiffets you aren't capable of concentrating for more than thirty-three minutes at a time? Is that it? My dear, it makes no sense. If you had porch steps that needed fixing and a shed that needed painting and a lawn to mow, would you spend thirty-three minutes fixing the steps and then go paint for thirty-three minutes and drop your brushes and go mow the grass for thirty-three minutes? No, you wouldn't. You'd mow the whole lawn and then fix the steps. And then you'd stop and eat cookies and drink some lemonade for a good long time. And tomorrow you'd start painting the shed."

The class giggled. Even Simon allowed himself a smile. Aunt Mattie definitely had a way of making you see things differently.

"Imagine if grown-ups ran *their* lives that way," said Matilda sternly. "What would that be like?"

Moses, a boy who had never stuck his hand up before, raised his hand now. "It would be like if your mother got halfway through the grocery shopping and she left her cart in the middle of the aisle because it's time to go do laundry."

Mollie stuck up her hand. "Or, you'd call the police

because a burglar is breaking into your home," she said, giggling. "And the policeman would arrive and look at his watch and he'd be like, 'Sorry, lady, can't stay, I have to go direct traffic now for the next thirty-three minutes.' "

"Or you call the fire department because your house is on fire," offered Mandy, "and they get halfway there and then turn around because it's time for washing the fire truck."

By this time the whole class was laughing. Matilda held up her hands for silence.

"I think you get the picture. In my class, at any rate, we work on something until it's done. Understood? Now then, where were we? Mollie, can you tell me why the bell is not ringing?"

Mollie looked at the diagram, looked at the bell. "Because you broke the circuit?" she said.

"Exactly," said Matilda. The sound next door had changed to the muffled tones of the PA. "Would you like to demonstrate to us how that works?"

Mollie looked uncertain.

"Go ahead," urged Mattie. "Climb right up there."

So Mollie climbed onto the chair, picked up one of the dangling PA wires, peered for a few seconds at the box, looked at the diagram on the blackboard, and stuck the wire into the box. Instantly the voice of Mr. Lister could be heard.

"—please rise for—" Mollie pulled the wire out and then in and out again, with the result that Mr. Lister's voice came across in quick staccato bursts: "—ledge of Alleg . . . the fla . . . United Sta . . . merica—" The class

cheered, and Mollie climbed down, made a brief bow to the class, and took her seat. Simon, sitting next to Julie, saw her nudge Mandy in the ribs. Mandy tried to ignore her.

"Very good," said Matilda, returning to her desk. "And now that you all understand electrical circuits, let us move on to the porcupine quill." She pulled the quill from her pocket just as Julie hissed, "Go on!" at Mandy. "The quill—" Mattie began, but stopped when she saw a raised hand. "Yes, Mandy," she said, with just the tiniest hint of irritation.

"We're supposed to do the Pledge of a Legions now," said Mandy, with a look at Julie.

"We *have* to," said Julie.

"Yeah," said Raggie. "Or we'll be arrested or something. For being *quislings*," he added brightly.

"Oh my," said Matilda. "Well, we can't have that. Very well, proceed."

The children rose dutifully, faced a flag in the corner of the room, and placed their hands in what they imagined to be the general area of their hearts.

"I plejuleejunz," droned the class in dull, sing-song voices. They mumbled along to the end and sat down with a clatter of chairs.

Matilda looked at them. "Everyone take out a piece of paper," she commanded. The class stared at her. "A piece of paper and a pencil." The students obeyed, mutely. "Now, would everyone please write down the Pledge of Allegiance."

As Simon worked, Julie nudged him. "It's your turn next," she whispered, without taking her eyes from her work. Simon looked at her blankly. "To interrupt her, stupid." But Simon had had time to think about the way he'd acted yesterday. It was one thing, he decided, to be unable to admit Mrs. Maxwell was his aunt; it was quite another thing to make fun of her and take part in Sink the Sub. He shook his head firmly and concentrated on his paper. Julie gave him a black look and then, while Aunt Mattie wasn't looking, wrote a note and passed it to Sebastian. Sebastian read it. He, too, shook his head.

Minutes later Matilda collected the papers, read

through them, and then faced the class. "Can anyone tell me what the Pledge of Allegiance means?" Silence. "Does anyone know what *allegiance* means?" The students looked at one another and shrugged. Julie glanced around the class and then put up her hand.

"Are we doing Social Studies now?" she asked.

"Yes, we're doing Social Studies," said Matilda tartly. "Whatever that means." She turned and, glancing through the students' papers, began to write on the board. This is what she wrote:

I pledge a legions to the flag of the Untied States of America. Undo the republic, for Richard Stands, one Asian, under God, invisible, with liberty, injustice for all.

"Does anybody have the faintest idea what that means? No? But you stand here day after day, year after year, with your hands firmly on your hearts, or what you imagine to be your hearts because I notice that most of you put your hands on your clavicle or possibly your pancreas, and you make a solemn promise. To protect liberty and 'injustice.' To be loyal to Richard Stands, whoever he might be. A mysterious Asian, it seems. An invisible Asian at that. Land sakes, children. Where do you park your brains when you come to school? Eh? Well, I guess we have our work cut out for us this morning, don't we?"

And that morning no one heard the bell for recess because they were busy figuring out who Richard Stands was.

Or maybe it was because the bell never rang.

Lemon Meringue Pi?

SCHOOL SCIENCE
FAIR
2 weeks left

After recess, Matilda pulled the quills out of her apron pocket and faced the class. Simon didn't want to be the one to do it, but somebody had to remind her. He stuck his hand up.

"The quill," began Aunt Matilda. She stopped. "Yes, Simon?"

"Excuse me," he said. "But we're supposed to be working on our Science Fair project now. There are only a few weeks left." At this the whole class groaned.

"Why don't you keep your mouth shut, Simon?" said Jimmy under his breath. "Thanks a whole lot."

Matilda looked thoughtful. "Yes, I suppose we should be thinking about the Science Fair. What is your project?"

Mollie trudged over to the corner of the room and picked up a huge scroll of white paper. Mandy helped her unroll it.

"Pi," said Mollie.

"Pie? That sounds fun. What kind of pie?"

"No, not that kind of pie. This kind of pi." Mollie and Mandy unrolled the paper. It spread all the way across

the blackboard and was covered with the biggest single long-division problem Matilda had ever seen. The answer to it, so far, was: 3.14159265358979323846264338 32795028841971693993751058209749445923078164 06286208998628034825334.

"Pi," explained Simon, "is how you get the circumference of a circle, or something like that. It's a fraction. No matter how far you divide it out, it keeps on going. On and on forever. No one's ever gotten to the end of it. Mrs. Biggs thought it would be fun to try figuring it out to a hundred places. We had to work on it every day. If we were bad, we worked on it extra."

"Oh my. And is it?"

"What?"

"Fun?"

Another groan was her answer.

"Are you learning anything by doing it?"

"How to die of boredom," said Jimmy. "Which we already knew."

"Yeah, see, Mrs. Biggs loves math. She went to MIT or something."

Aunt Mattie looked at the scroll. Then she went to her desk, opened drawers, and rummaged around for a moment. "What I don't understand," she said at last, "is why you don't just do this." And, producing a large calculator, she punched some numbers in. "There. That's your answer. Or close enough." She rolled up the pi scroll and put it in a closet.

The students looked at her, dumbfounded.

"Now, let's try to think up a more interesting science project. Ideas?"

Simon glanced around the class. No one seemed the least bit interested in the topic. Mario yawned. Sebastian began doodling on his homework assignment sheet. Mollie was whispering to Mindy, who had her head in a book.

"Come, come. Surely there's something we could do."

"What's the point?" said Jimmy. "We'll never win anything. Mr. Farley's class is going to win again. They always do. So why bother?"

"What are they doing?" asked Matilda.

"Nothing much. Just building a computer," said Jimmy. Everyone slumped in their desks at this reminder. "It's way cool. They've been working on it since school started. No way we can beat it."

"A computer? Fifth graders? Goodness me, how ambitious."

"Yeah, well, Wilton Pflummerfield is in that class."

"Who's he? A computer genius?" asked Matilda. The class burst into laughter.

"Let me put it this way," said Julie. "That boy is so dumb, he thinks chocolate milk comes from brown cows."

"You astonish me," said Mattie.

"He acts like he's smart—but he's not," explained Ethan.

"The lights may be burning," continued Julie, "but nobody's home. The TV's on, but it's not plugged in, if you get my drift."

"The monitor's working, but the hard drive ain't," said Mario, getting into the spirit. Simon could see that Julie was on a roll, and she had the rest of the class with her again.

"Yeah," said Mindy. "It's a big fat book, but the pages are all blank."

"His elevator," said Bix, "doesn't go all the way to the top floor."

Mattie stopped them. "I think I get the picture," she said. "He's not the brightest star in the sky, poor child. But how does that help his class with—"

"His dad is *Mr. Pflummerfield*," said Simon, trying to help Aunt Mattie out.

"Of course he is," said Matilda. "Stands to reason that Wilton Pflummerfield's dad would be called Mr. Pflummerfield." Simon sighed.

"Pflummerfield," repeated Julie patiently, as Matilda showed no signs of recognition. "As in Pflummerfield Home Computing. Pflummerfield Electronics & Engi-

neering. The big computer makers? Everybody's heard of them, unless they've been on Mars or someplace."

Aunt Mattie simply shrugged at this, and Simon could practically hear the other students concluding that, yes, she obviously *had* been on Mars or someplace. After all, she thought the Chicago Bulls were a meat-packing plant.

"The point is," she said, "why would anyone *want* to build a computer for the Science Fair? There are far too many computers in the world already. Do we really need another? No, no," she continued, answering her own question, "we must think of something more original. More useful. Something the world does need. Not another computer." She smiled at the class. "We will come up with the most exciting Science Fair project in years, I can feel it."

The class did not appear to share her enthusiasm. There was a glum silence.

"I guess nobody told you," said Mario at last. "We're the stupid class. We're not good at anything. And we're worst at math and science."

"Rubbish," said Mrs. Maxwell. "Everyone's good at something."

"It's not rubbish, Mrs. Maxwell," said Mindy. "We're the only class in the school that has never even won a Math Bee. If we can't win a crummy Math Bee, how can we win the County Science Fair?"

"Well," said Matilda, surveying the gloomy class, "the answer is very clear. We will start by winning the Math Bee." She tossed the calculator back in the drawer and smiled broadly. "Whatever that is."

Oops

$$76 \times 54 =$$
$$127 \div 13 =$$

It fell to Simon to explain to Aunt Mattie the details of the Math Bee. It was lunchtime, and Simon found himself, once again, sitting alone. (Well, not exactly alone, but to Simon's mind, fifth-grade girls didn't really count.) And then Aunt Mattie came, with her brown lunch bag, and sat herself down at the end of the long table. Today, Simon noticed, she was wearing the other pair of mismatched shoes, and enormously long, dangly earrings. At least the earrings matched.

The Math Bee, Simon explained, in answer to Aunt Mattie's question, had been Mrs. Biggs's idea of a *really* fun time. "She'd get teams from all the fourth or fifth grades or whoever together in the auditorium," he went on. "It's sort of like one of those old TV quiz shows, where they had college teams competing against each other. The whole school watches."

"You'll get to see for yourself," said Mollie with a sigh. "Fifth grades are having one this Friday."

"Five kids from each class sit up on the stage," continued Simon. "Mrs. Biggs fires math problems at them as fast as she can: What's 76 times 54? Or 127 divided

by 13? The first kid to get the right answer wins points for the team. Wrong answers cost you points."

"And what do you win?" asked Matilda.

"Usually the team—the class—gets to take a day off from school to go on some field trip or other," said Mandy.

"Well, that could come in handy," mused Matilda, looking around at the students. "Yes, that's a very nice prize for a Math Bee."

The word *prize* must have caught Mr. Farley's ear as he walked by, for he stopped. "The Math Bee prize?" he asked. "You don't imagine *you're* going to win, do you?" The students were already picking up their trays and lunch boxes—they ate in a matter of nano-seconds—and perhaps that's why Mr. Farley didn't bother to lower his voice. But Matilda spoke up, loud enough to cause the students to stop and listen.

"Oh, no," she said. "I don't *imagine* we're going to win."

"Good," said Mr. Farley. "Because—"

"I *know* we're going to win." Charley Farley threw his head back and snorted with amusement. This made him look so much like a seal Simon could hardly stand it. He should be balancing a ball on the end of his nose right now, he thought.

"Can't miss, dearie," continued Aunt Mattie. She gave Simon a conspiratorial wink. "I have a secret weapon."

"Sure you do," said Mr. Farley, still laughing. "You're going to feed your kids toxic waste and turn them into Teenage Mutant Math Champs. Hey, speaking of prizes, have you had a chance to work on that Science Fair

71

project yet? You know, the Giant Pi in the Sky? Now there's a real winner, eh?" He laughed and patted Matilda on the shoulder.

"Oh, we've abandoned the pi project," said Aunt Mattie. "We're starting a new one."

"With only two weeks to go until the fair? What is it?"

"We don't know yet. But it'll be a winner. Won't it, Simon?" She ignored Mr. Farley's snort of disbelief. "And how is your project going?"

"We're going to amaze them this year." He smiled expansively. "I wouldn't be surprised if we went on to win the State—no, the National—Science Fair. Imagine, a working computer!"

"And all done by fifth graders?" asked Aunt Mattie innocently. "All by themselves?"

Mr. Farley just laughed. "Smartest darn fifth graders you ever saw," he said, with a wink at the two of them. "Especially that Pflummerfield boy."

Simon was waiting in line behind Raggie to scrape his uneaten meal into the garbage when Miss Boynton came up to Aunt Mattie as she was leaving the cafeteria.

"How are you doing, dear?" Miss Boynton asked, raising her eyebrows in a way that could only mean: Ready to shoot yourself yet?

"Fine, just fine," said Aunt Mattie. "Quite an engaging group of youngsters."

"Are you aware you've set a school record?"

"Indeed? In what way?"

"Two whole days and not a single child sent to Mr. Bickle's office. A record for a substitute in that class. Have you handed out any warnings? Mrs. Biggs used to hand them out with a shovel—especially to poor Raggie and that Jimmy."

"Why, yes, I've given out quite a few, mostly to myself, though: for being late, forgetting to send attendance sheets in, and so on."

Miss Boynton raised her eyebrows in surprise. "Indeed? Well, if your Raggie gets many more warnings, he's in major trouble. He just got one from Mr. Farley for not having a hall pass."

Simon shot a look at Raggie, but Raggie didn't appear to be listening to the conversation.

"Does that mean he has to stay after school Tuesday?"

"Yes. And one more detention, and he's out of here. Suspended."

"Oh dear," said Aunt Mattie to herself. "I'll have to start passing out more warnings, then." And she hastened out into the hall, leaving Miss Boynton shaking her head in amazement.

At that moment Simon received a shove from the rear. Ethan and Jimmy were behind him with their lunch trays. "Did you have a nice lunch with the teacher?" sneered Jimmy. "I see you're back to being teacher's pet."

"Sucking up, as usual," said Ethan disgustedly. Then, before Simon could reply, they shouldered past him and Raggie, and as they did so, the leftover spaghetti

from Jimmy's tray somehow spilled onto Simon and Raggie.

"Oops," snickered Jimmy, and turned his back.

Raggie looked down at his ruined clothes. "I'm dead," he said.

Simon looked at his own neat white shirt, now stained tomato red. And then, before he knew what he was doing, he had upended his tray on Jimmy's head.

Dangerously Slippery

"An accident, you say?"

Jimmy nodded. He appeared a little disconcerted. Maybe it was the bits of spaghetti still clinging to his ear. Or maybe he just wasn't used to talking to someone who was knitting.

"Yeah," he managed to say. "I just like bumped into him and everything spilled. By accident." He shot Simon a defiant look.

"Simon? Is that what happened?" Aunt Mattie glanced up from her knitting, giving Simon a distracted look, and said, "Knit one, purl two."

"He—" It was a simple act, but one that Simon had never done before. He had never lied. Ever. "Yes, he must have slipped."

"And how did *your* tray end up on *his* head? Knit two, purl one, cast off."

"I don't remember, it just sort of—"

"He slipped, too," said Jimmy.

"I see. And you, Raggie? Do you have anything to say?"

Raggie, staring at the floor, just shook his head.

Silence, but for the sound of knitting needles clicking softly.

"Jimmy, how many detentions do you have so far this year?"

"Three."

"Two more and you get suspended?"

"Yeah, so, big whoop."

"Will your parents think it's a big whoop?"

"They don't care," said Jimmy. "They probably won't even notice. They're too busy going to basketball games and piano recitals."

"What about you, Raggie? You have four detentions?"

Raggie nodded. He ducked his chin, pulled the edge of his T-shirt up into his mouth and started chewing on it. His T-shirts were all raggedy from his chewing on them all the time.

"And if you get suspended, what happens? Does your family notice?" There was a long silence while Raggie gnawed his T-shirt. "Knit two, purl two," said Aunt Mattie to her needles. Then Raggie wiped his nose with the back of his wrist.

"My dad," he said in a whisper, "will kill me."

The needles stopped their clicking. Aunt Mattie rummaged around in her suitcase of a purse and produced a small bottle labeled Surefire Llama Spit Stain Remover. "Well, then, I suggest you go clean up. Take this. It not only vaporizes llama spit, but is guaranteed to send spaghetti stains packing as well." Raggie nodded, grabbed the bottle, and vanished. Mattie turned back to Simon and Jimmy.

"In the future, try to watch where you're going,

especially when carrying spaghetti. The floors in this school appear to be dangerously slippery. By the way," she added, "I'm pairing up children in the class to work on the Science Fair project. You three boys will be a team. I want you to move your desks together." Simon and Jimmy looked at each other wordlessly. Finally Aunt Mattie spoke again.

"I'm worried about young Raggie. We must do everything we can to keep him from getting suspended—not just for his sake, but for the whole class's. I have a hunch he may be very helpful with this Science Fair project. I need someone who will look out for him." She looked at Simon, who was about to speak. But before he could open his mouth, her glance slid right past him to Jimmy.

"Jimmy," she said, "I want you to be his guardian angel. Can you do that? Can you keep Raggie out of trouble, keep an eye on our little escape artist? Kind of like a big brother?"

Simon saw the surprise in Jimmy's eyes and felt, with the force of total certainty, that no one had ever asked him to do anything like this before. He saw Jimmy wrestling with the question. He could practically hear him thinking: Hey, this is not cool. And, What about Sink the Sub? And, Who cares about the dumb Science Fair?

And he saw that it surprised Jimmy as much as anyone else when he answered, "I dunno. Maybe. Yeah, I could do that, I guess."

"Good," said Aunt Mattie crisply. "See that you do. Never let him out of your sight. He's a regular Houdini, he is. Why, he's probably halfway to New York right now." Her needles resumed their clicking. Her fingers flew over the wool. "Cast off," she said. And the two boys left, though they couldn't be sure if she was talking to them, or to her knitting.

The Secret Weapon

Aunt Mattie brought the class to attention the next morning by taking Runcible out of her cage and letting the parrot sit on her shoulder.

"Shut up!" said Runcible, sidling along Mattie's shoulder. She cocked her head and looked at the students. "Shut up please."

The noisy class quieted down.

"As you know," Matilda told them, "we have only two days until the Math Bee."

"I can't wait," said Julie.

Matilda ignored her. "We need to win the Math Bee, and to do that I've decided to bring in a math coach."

"You got a math genius to come coach us?" asked Ethan, incredulous. "How'd you do that?"

"What is he, a college professor or something?" asked Mollie.

Mattie smiled. "You remember I told you I had a secret weapon? I brought it with me today. Please meet my secret weapon."

She opened the door and gestured to someone in the

hall. A moment later, a lanky man with a silvery mustache and longish silvery hair stepped into the room.

"Wow. Albert Einstein," said one student.

"Looks just like him," said another.

Simon closed his eyes. It didn't look like Albert Einstein to him. It looked just like Uncle Philbert. Exactly like his great-uncle Philbert.

Maybe if he kept his eyes closed long enough, things would change. When he opened them again, Uncle Philbert would no longer be standing at the front of his class, reeking of barn, with little bits of hay sticking to his hair, his baggy farm overalls, his Bob's Feed Lot baseball hat. Sometimes wishes did come true, you know, if you closed your eyes and wished hard enough.

"Class, meet Mr. Philbert Maxwell," said Aunt Mattie to the students. And to Philbert she said, "Bertie, dear, we don't wear caps in the classroom."

"Are you a nuclear physicist?" asked Mario.

"No, sir," said Philbert pulling off his hat and picking some straw out of his mustache. "I'm a farmer."

There was an audible groan throughout the class. Students who had been sitting alertly in their seats slumped back in their chairs. Simon, who been slumping back in his chair to start with, slumped even lower. So much for wishing it all away. Never mind, he had a better plan: He could fake his own death. He would hold his breath for so long that he'd turn purple and they would call an ambulance and take him to a hospital. Preferably in Timbuktu.

"Excuse me," said Julie. "But why is a farmer coming

to coach us in arithmetic? Are you some sort of math brain?"

"Nope," said Philbert. "I hate math. Hated going to school. Hated all that stuff."

"Which is why he is the perfect person to *teach* you math," said Aunt Mattie. "I myself am quite good at math. Which means I'm no good at teaching it."

"Why?"

"Because, if you're very good at something, you can never understand people who have a hard time with it. Can't understand why they just don't get it."

"That's Mrs. Biggs," said Julie under her breath.

"No, what you need is not me but someone like Philbert."

"What you need," corrected Philbert, "is MultiQwik, Uncle Philbert's Patented Homework-Reducing Time-Saving Three-Step Multiple-Digit Multiplication Method.

"You see," he explained, "when I was your age, I hated wasting time on homework. Especially when there was really important stuff to be done, like collecting horse chestnuts or making turtle traps. So one day, kinda by accident, I discovered a much quicker way to do multiplication. It got me in a lot of trouble in school, because first they thought I was cheatin', then when they saw I wasn't cheatin' they got all upset. Decided my method was too different. They were scared of stuff that wasn't in their textbooks. So they didn't allow me to use it in school. But it sure made the homework go faster. And now I'm going to teach it to you."

"Do you need a computer?"

"How does it work?"

The class bombarded him with questions, but Philbert just shook his head.

"Hang on, young whiffets. Ask me a multiplication question. Two digits. Go ahead."

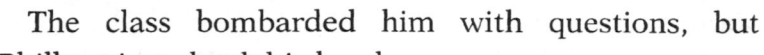

Mario pulled out a calculator. "Okay," he said. "What's 32 times 23?"

"Easy," said Philbert. "It's 736. Next question?"

"He's right," whispered Mario.

"What's 45 times 28?"

"Let's see." This time Philbert wrote the two numbers on the board, but instead of multiplying them out, he just looked at them. "I'm a little rusty," he explained. "That would be 1,260."

"Right again," said Mario. Simon let out his breath in a rush. The kids around him stopped fidgeting and sat up again in their seats. He decided to postpone dying for a little bit.

"Next question."

"What's up, doc?" (That was Runcible, and everyone ignored her, for once.)

"Can you do three digits?" asked Mario.

"Try me," said Philbert.

A half hour later, Uncle Philbert brushed the chalk dust off his hands, retrieved his cap, and faced Aunt Mattie.

"What do you think? Will they be able to do it?"

"I don't know," she said. "But at least now we've got a fighting chance. The proof, as they say, is in the pudding."

And the pudding, thought Simon, is the day after tomorrow. He looked around at the kids in his class. Not a lot of time to get ready. Not a lot of time at all.

To Bee or Not to Bee

$$165 \div 15 = ?$$
$$230 \div 12 = ?$$

The three fifth grades filed slowly into the auditorium ahead of the rest of the school and arranged themselves in the front rows. The teachers stood in groups at the rear of the room. As class monitor, Simon, too, stood at the rear of the room, for it was his job to do the overhead lights. Presently five students from each fifth-grade class climbed up onto the stage and took seats at one of three long tables. In the center of the stage was a blackboard, and Mr. Bickle, the principal, stood in front of it holding a sheaf of notes.

A few feet from Simon, Mr. Farley was whispering to Otis Lister. "Something's up," he said in a low voice.

"What do you mean?" asked the assistant principal.

"Look at that class, Mrs. Biggs's class. They're acting funny."

Simon looked. It was true. Instead of their habitual slouching, bored attitude, Mrs. Biggs's—Aunt Mattie's—students had exchanged high fives and were now making the thumbs-up sign to the five members of their class walking onto the stage.

"That's not possible. What is she thinking of?" Farley continued.

"What?"

"Look! Look at the kids she's picked for the Math Bee. I've got my best guys up there. But she's got—and where's Simon? He's the only smart kid in the class. He's not even up there. Sheesh. This is gonna be painful." He smirked.

Simon shrank back against the wall, hoping they wouldn't notice him. He thought back to the moment when Aunt Mattie had selected the math team. Simon had automatically stood up, pencil and paper in hand. He'd been on every Math Bee team this year.

"No, Simon, sit down," Aunt Mattie had said, looking around. "I think we'll have, let's see, Jimmy and Mindy and Raggie and Mollie, and . . . *Julie.*" The looks on the faces of the five students had been almost comic: clearly they couldn't decide between shock, pride, and horror.

"Oh, goody," said Julie softly. "I just love public humiliation. It's so fun." For a long moment, Simon wondered if Julie would simply refuse to do it. He saw her look to Mollie and Mindy for support, but the two girls were bent over a sheet of paper. The other students were lining up to go.

"Come on," Simon had whispered to her. "You can do this." He grabbed a calculator. "I'll quiz you on the way." Julie had given him a look, half gratitude, half disbelief.

"This," she said as she snatched a pencil from her desk, "this is what you get when you have a fruitcake for a teacher."

85

Raggie, too, had looked terrified at being picked, and halfway to the auditorium he tried to bolt. But Jimmy collared him and dragged him back. "Cut it out, you little punk," he said fiercely. "If I can get up on that stage and make a fool out of myself, so can you. Besides," he added, "rocket scientists are supposed to be good at math."

Now here they all were, traipsing onto the stage, still looking slightly dazed, but definitely cheered by their classmates' show of confidence in them.

Mr. Bickle stood up to announce the rules of the Math Bee. Simon flicked the auditorium lights off and the stage lights on.

"As you know, the first person to . . . when you get the answer, as soon as you, you stand up and announce the answer. Five points for every correct answer, and two points off for every wrong, um, every one that's . . . Today we're doing division and multiplication. The winner is . . . the first team to get to one hundred is the, um . . . Are you ready?"

The students all nodded.

"Okay, here we . . . um . . . let's get . . . First question: 165 divided by 15 is . . . ?"

For the next fifteen minutes, as Mr. Bickle peppered them with long-division questions, Mr. Farley's and Miss Frescobaldi's teams battled it out.

"Look at that!" said Farley. "Mrs. Maxwell's class hasn't gotten a single answer—not a single point. This is embarrassing."

"You're wrong," hissed Mr. Lister. "They've gotten four points. *Minus* four points!" It was true. Mindy and Mollie had each tried to answer a question—with disastrous results. Still, the five of them sat up there looking remarkably calm. At the end of the first round of twenty questions, the score was Mr. Farley's class forty-eight points, Miss Frescobaldi's forty-two points, Matilda's minus six.

"Now we come to, it's time for the second half of, of . . ." announced Mr. Bickle. "Multiplication. Question number one: What is 43 times 12?"

Mindy stood up. At the other tables, students still busy scribbling on paper looked at her in surprise. Simon held his breath.

"Yes, Mindy?" said Mr. Bickle. "Are you, that is to say, do you have a question?"

"No," said Mindy. "I have an answer. Five hundred and sixteen." She sat down. Everyone stared, dumbfounded. Mr. Bickle consulted his notes. "Correct," he said slowly. "Very good, Mindy." He was too polite to say "Lucky guess," but Charley Farley wasn't.

"Dumb luck," said Mr. Farley with a laugh to Otis Lister. "Nearly lost the team another two points."

"Next question," continued Mr. Bickle: "What is 34 times 71?" This time there was a brief pause. Raggie jotted a few numbers on a sheet of paper and looked at Jimmy. "Go for it," muttered Jimmy. Raggie stood up. Once again, the other students stopped scribbling to stare.

"Can I help you, Raggie?" asked Mr. Bickle.

"No," said Raggie. "Two thousand four hundred and fourteen."

He sat down. Mr. Bickle consulted his notes.

"Correct," he said slowly, an astonished look on his face. "Raggie, that's, that's quite . . ."

"That's cheating, that's what it is," shouted Mr. Farley. "Nobody could get the right answer that fast." This time he said it so the whole auditorium could hear him.

"All right," said Mr. Bickle. "Quiet please"—for everyone was talking, including all the contestants. The only ones who were quiet were the five students from Matilda's class. They sat silently at their table, hands folded. Raggie and Mindy were even smiling and looking the tiniest bit smug.

"Next question: What is 84 times 79?"

This time it was Julie who stood up. Why'd she have to pick such a hard one? thought Simon. For the first time since he'd known her, she looked nervous in front of a crowd. Simon gave her a discreet thumbs-up and mouthed *Go on* at her. "Six thousand six hundred thirty-six," she said, and sat down. Simon checked his calculator: 6,636.

This time the auditorium erupted into cheers and shouts. Matilda's class was on its feet clapping. Mr. Farley ran down the aisle and bounded onto the stage.

"They're cheating," he announced. "Someone's got a calculator." To Mr. Bickle he said, "She told me she had a secret weapon."

But a quick search of the table revealed nothing but some paper and pencils—no secret weapon. Still Mr. Farley persisted. "Let me see your work," he said. "Look! There isn't any work. I told you they're cheating. They didn't even multiply the problem out. They just wrote down the answer." He held up a sheet. Indeed, he was right: Mindy's page contained nothing, not even the problem. Julie's and Raggie's contained only the problem written down, with the answer under it. "Someone must have copied your question sheet. They memorized the answers."

"Well, if you like I'll . . ." said Mr. Bickle, "I won't use my . . . I'll make up the next question on the, on the . . ."

"On the spot!" finished Mr. Lister for him. He, too, had climbed up on stage.

"And we'll have Mrs. Maxwell's class do the question

right here at the board," insisted Farley. "That way no one can possibly cheat."

Mr. Farley took a seat on the stage. Julie, Jimmy, Raggie, Mindy, and Mollie trooped obediently up to the blackboard.

"Okay, children," said Mr. Bickle, taking out a calculator, "the next problem is, um, let's see, 24 times 37." Simultaneously, Matilda's students wrote the problem on the board, while the others worked at their tables. More or less simultaneously, they all wrote the answer under the problem, without going through any of the usual steps for multiplying large numbers.

"I don't understand at all how you, what you . . ." said Mr. Bickle. "But you have all, you're all correct. You may sit down."

And so it went. Mr. Farley was, at last, speechless. Mr. Bickle rattled off the next questions, all made up on the spot. The students from Matilda's class were always first to answer, and were correct on all but two problems. Even when one of them got one wrong, someone else on the team jumped up with the right answer long before any other team was ready. Mr. Farley's class began making desperate attempts at wild guesses, only to lose points. When it was all over, Mattie's class had neatly beaten the others by more than fifty points. It was a rout.

And Mr. Farley's class had come in last.

Simon stood by the door waiting for the jubilant class to file out of the auditorium. Jimmy and Raggie walked by, both of them grinning. "Way to go," said

Simon. Raggie gave him a shy smile, and Jimmy turned and gave him a high five.

"Yeah," he said. "Way to go."

Simon was suddenly aware of Miss Frescobaldi, hovering by his side. She drew him away from the crowd of students.

"What's your secret weapon?" she asked Simon in a whisper. Even Miss Frescobaldi, it seemed, could not help feeling that some kind of, well, cheating must have gone on. So Simon explained to her, with the aid of a piece of paper and a pencil, Uncle Philbert's Patented Homework-Reducing Time-Saving Three-Step Multiple-Digit Multiplication Method.

"No secret weapon," he said. "Anyone can do it. Give me a problem."

"Um, 32 times 31," said Miss Frescobaldi. Simon nodded and wrote the following on the paper:

1. multiply	2. multiply and add results	3. multiply
3 **2**	**3 2**	3 2
↕	✕	↕
x3 **1**	**x3 1**	**x3** 1
2	**9** 2	**9**92

"First you multiply the right-hand column of figures—that is the 2 and the 1. You get 2. Then you multiply each number diagonally and add them: so it's 1x3 plus 3x2, which equals 9. Then you multiply the left-hand column of figures: 3x3, which equals 9. There's your answer: 992. It gets a little harder if you have to

carry a number, but you do that just like in adding. With a little practice you can do it all in your head, without any paper at all."

"How revolutionary," said Miss Frescobaldi. "I'm going to try it on my students right away. It's so easy!"

"Not to mention," said Simon, grinning, "extremely proficuous."

"So," he said to Julie when he finally caught up with the class. "You still think she's a fruitcake?"

"I'll give her this much," said Julie. "She's smart. A very smart fruitcake. But still a fruitcake. And Philbert's a nut." She looked around. "Get it? A *filbert* is a kind of nut. Hello? You're supposed to laugh, people."

But no one did. Julie's joke seemed forced, as if her heart wasn't really in it. And everyone else was busy talking about the Math Bee and making fun of the expressions on the faces of Mr. Farley and his class. Perhaps, thought Simon, laughing at subs had become old; but gloating about winning—now *that* was something new and different!

No Respect

Mr. Lister and Mr. Farley walked silently down the hall to Mr. Lister's office.

"Come into my office for a minute, Charley," said the assistant principal. He shut the door firmly behind them. "We've got to do something about that Maxwell woman," he said the moment the door clicked shut. "She has no respect for rules or authority. And she is making a mockery of school discipline, setting a terrible example for the children."

Mr. Farley nodded absently. "That Math Bee," he said. "She had to have cheated."

"I can't decide who is worse—that impossible woman, or our fearless leader Herbert J. Bickle, who refuses to sack her."

"I don't know," said Farley, smoothing back his dark hair. "You can't fire someone for winning a Math Bee." This was not the first time he had listened to Otis Lister complain about Mrs. Maxwell, or Mr. Bickle.

"They've got to go," sputtered Lister. "Both of them. And it's to your advantage, Charley, to see that they do go." This got Mr. Farley's attention.

"How so?" he asked, sitting up straight.

Mr. Lister swiveled his chair so that he was looking out the window.

"Imagine if you will—just hypothetically now—that Mr. Herbert J. Bickle was, unexpectedly, to lose his job. And imagine if you will that"—he cleared his throat a bit—"that Assistant Principal Otis T. Lister took his place. Well, that would leave open the job of assistant principal, wouldn't it? And *Principal* Otis T. Lister"—this had such a nice ring to it, he said it again—"Principal Otis T. Lister could think of someone who would make a very *good* assistant principal. Someone covered with the glory of winning yet another science fair, for example."

He spun his chair and looked straight at Mr. Farley, who jumped up and began to pace.

"Yes!" exclaimed Farley. "Someone who had brought honor—and prizes—showering down upon the school!"

"A proven winner," concluded Lister solemnly.

Mr. Farley stopped pacing. "But how?" he asked. "How do we get rid of Bickle?"

"Bickle is away next Wednesday," said Otis. "And while the cat's away . . ."

"What are you planning?"

"I happen to know that the superintendent of schools will be here that day. I've arranged for a special assembly, and I'm going to give a speech. I'm working on it right now." He patted a pile of papers on his desk. "It will display Herbert Bickle and Otis Lister in their true light." He straightened himself and gazed grandly out the window. Charley Farley could see that he was rehearsing some of the lines of that speech in his head. Otis Lister smiled and nodded to an imaginary audience. His lips moved silently. Suddenly the smile vanished and he returned to earth. "But that won't take care of the Maxwell woman. How are we to get rid of her?"

Mr. Farley had a quick inspiration. "Why are we worrying ourselves about her?" he asked. "The kids in her class will take care of her for us. They always do. I heard several of them placing bets on how many days she would last. No sub has ever lasted more than a week with that class."

"I hope you're right."

"I'm always right, Otis," he said with a laugh. "Trust me."

What the World Needs Now

"Well, we know we can win a Math Bee," said Aunt Mattie, regarding the class. "Now, on to the Science Fair. Let us find a project worthy of this class."

The students were still buzzing with pleasure and excitement at having won the Bee. But the mention of the Science Fair created complete silence.

"Julie, what do you like?"

"Huh?" said Julie. "What's that got to do with science? I'm no good at science. I hate it."

"Just like you're no good at math? Answer the question. Tell me what you *are* good at."

Julie made a face at Mindy. "Okay. Acting. Want to see my impersonation of Mr. Bickle?" She jumped up.

"I'd love to," said Matilda, making a note, "some other time, thank you. Now, Mindy. What do you like?"

"I like to write." Matilda noted this down.

"Mario? What are you good at?"

Mario raised his head from his desk and yawned. "Sleeping," he said. This got a laugh, but Matilda noted it down anyway.

"Moses?"

"Well," said Moses slowly, and a grin split his wide, round face. "Eating. Food. I like cooking and eating."

"Good. Sebastian?"

"I like to draw."

"Ethan?"

"I dunno. Building stuff, I guess. I like Legos."

"Raggie?"

"Rockets," said Raggie. "Real rockets."

And so it went around the room. Mandy liked her pet guinea pigs. Mollie liked rock music. Jimmy liked rocks. Bix liked basketball. At last she came to Simon.

"Simon, what do you like?"

"Math, I guess."

"Math. Anything else?"

"And my cat, Raspberry."

Aunt Mattie looked up.

"I see." There was a pause as she looked down at her notes. "Well, you all have a lot of things you're good at or you like. Which brings me to the last question: What do you hate?"

"That's easy," said Mario with another yawn. "Getting up in the morning."

"Yeah," chorused other students.

"And eating breakfast," added Mandy. "It's always the same thing—cold cereal."

"All right," said Matilda briskly. "This makes things easy. The world may not need another computer, but it clearly needs something to make it easier to get up in the morning and eat breakfast. Your assignment, then,

for the weekend, is to design a machine, using the things you do like, to help with the things you don't like.

"Now let us turn to vocabulary. Who here knows what *pecksniffian* means? Nobody? What about *muculent*? Good. Write a definition for both of them."

The Mighty Muculent Egg Machine

Simon, his head bent over the desk, was grappling with the ignition problem, along with Raggie and Jimmy. Sebastian stood at the blackboard, drawing furiously as all around him students called out instructions. It was Monday morning, and Mrs. Maxwell was nowhere to be seen.

"It's going to be like *Scrambled Eggs Super*," said Mindy, waving the Dr. Seuss book in the air. "Only more super."

"It has to be taller, make it taller, Sebastian, so the eggs will break," said Ethan. "You need a ramp there, with a big drop."

"But what about the music?" asked Mollie. "How does that turn on?"

"Simple," said Jimmy. "Raggie's figured it out."

Raggie stood up bashfully. "With a rocket," he said.

"What?" shouted everyone, so Raggie ran to the board and demonstrated.

"Cool," said Ethan, and suddenly the whole class was talking at once. When at last Aunt Mattie walked in, a full forty-five minutes late, she was greeted with cries of

"We've got it!" and "We're ready," and "We're gonna blow them away!"

"Quiet, please," interrupted Matilda. "Everyone take your seats." Quiet—or something resembling quiet— fell, and the tangled mob of children gradually sorted itself into students who were more or less sitting at their desks.

"How does your corporosity seem to gashiate this morning?"

As usual there was no answer to this question, so she continued. "What have you been doing while I was late? Something interesting, I trust. Who would like to go first? Simon?"

"Go on, Simon," shouted Jimmy. "You explain it."

Simon stood up. "Well," he began, "we've thought up a project. For the Science Fair. Using the stuff we talked about on Friday—you know, using the stuff we like, to make something that solves a problem."

Aunt Mattie raised her eyebrows. "Indeed?"

"Yes," said Simon, and went to the front of the room. He picked up the pointer Mrs. Biggs had used for geography lessons. "It's called The Mighty Muculent Egg-Breaking and Breakfast-Making Morning-Waking Machine."

"I thought up the name," said Mindy.

"And the starring part will be played by *moi*," said Julie. She bowed to an imaginary audience. "Thank you, thank you very much."

"Please, Simon, go on."

"Here's how it works." Simon pointed to Sebastian's drawing on the blackboard and began to explain, using

broad gestures and trying to ignore the students who
interrupted him over and over, afraid he'd missed an
important part.

"Well, I never," said Aunt Mattie when he was done.
"Have you left anything out?"

"I don't think so," said Simon.

Matilda glanced at the notes she had taken on Friday.
"Except possibly guinea pigs," she said. She smiled at
the students. "And I'm sure you can find a way to fit
them in."

Work began on the Mighty Muculent Egg Machine that
very week—but not in the way Simon or anyone else
had expected.

On Monday afternoon Mrs. Maxwell gave out warnings to everyone in the class who didn't already have them—for not being late enough that morning, she explained. A howl of protest erupted from everyone but Raggie.

"Two warnings!"

"Not fair!"

"We'll have to stay after school tomorrow."

"Yes, you will!" said Matilda happily. "I'm staying, too, of course: I've got three warnings, but I'm willing to share mine if somebody didn't get enough. Now, who will bring the popcorn?"

"Popcorn?"

"Yes. I myself will bring some of my famous raspberry-butterscotch cookies. And lemonade. I don't approve of soda. Now, then, volunteers for popcorn?"

As had happened so often in the last five days, the class regarded Mrs. Maxwell speechlessly.

"Why?" asked Jimmy at last.

"Why? For the party, of course," said Matilda. "You can't have a Detention Party without food. I would have thought that was obvious."

"Detention Party?"

"Yes, of course. Well, we can't let Raggie be the only one who gets to stay after school, can we? I'm sorry, Raggie, but you must share the fun with others."

A huge grin was spreading across Raggie's thin face.

"A party?" he said. "Cool. A party!"

"Yes," said Matilda. She glanced round the classroom. "And maybe—if you're good—maybe I'll let you all

work on the Science Fair project. But only if you're good."

Mr. Farley shut the door to Otis Lister's office. "They've finally gotten to her," he said with a laugh. "Yes, she'll crack yet. Any day now."

"Why do you say that?" asked the assistant principal. "She looks quite cheerful every time I see her. Maddeningly cheerful. Horribly, infuriatingly cheerful."

Mr. Farley held up a fistful of pink slips. He flourished them in Mr. Lister's face. "Warnings. Detentions. She's been handing them out like confetti. Oh, yes. Any day now, she'll snap. I'm always right, Otis old boy. Did I mention to you that I'm always right? Why, the only time I've ever been known to be wrong was once in 1996 when I thought I had made a mistake—but I was mistaken." He laughed loudly. "Trust me on this, Otis. Just trust me."

Measure Twice, Cut Once

That Tuesday after school was to be the Detention Party.

Aunt Mattie brought the raspberry-butterscotch cookies that Simon remembered so well. And lemonade. Not regular yellow lemonade, or even pink lemonade, but blue lemonade because, as she explained, why not?

Bix and Julie brought trash bags filled with popcorn. Raggie brought rocket fuses and brownies he had convinced his older sisters to bake for him. Ethan brought a huge box of Legos. Moses brought eggs and a frying pan. Mandy brought her guinea pig. Jimmy brought his rock collection. Other children brought lumber scrounged from garages, hammers and tenpenny nails, pulleys, string, CD players, remote controls, eggbeaters, mixing bowls, batteries, wires, duct tape, and art supplies.

Outside, the sun was shining on a beautiful May day, but the children never once glanced out the window. They labored all afternoon on the Egg Machine. Matilda, who had a gift for machines (she had once,

Simon knew, rebuilt the engine of a 1946 New York taxicab all by herself) refused to participate. She claimed that this was the class's project and her role was to provide refreshments, encouragement, and first aid to children who insisted on hammering their fingernails instead of their tenpenny nails.

It was slow work, and frustrating. Simon, busy calculating the dimensions and angles of the machine, made a rare mathematical mistake and everyone had to redo a whole section.

"Measure twice, cut once," said Matilda from her desk, where she was peacefully knitting something that might have been a scarf for a smallish giraffe. "The motto of every good carpenter." And she said it more than once.

At another point, the structure, what little there was of it, collapsed under its own weight and needed to be completely rebuilt.

"Let us take a moment to consider how you calculate the weight-bearing capacity of the pulley," said Matilda. She went to the blackboard and drew some diagrams and formulas. The class watched silently while she explained. "Now have some lemonade, and start again."

By the end of the afternoon, two children had bandaged thumbs, three more had narrowly escaped stapling themselves to the floor, and almost all of them were covered in some combination of Elmer's glue, sawdust, and tempera paint. But a crude structure had taken shape on the floor of the classroom. It was far—very far—from being done. Nonetheless, it was an embryonic Egg Machine. Any fool could see that. Undeniably the beginning of the one and only Mighty Muculent Egg-Breaking and Breakfast-Making Morning-Waking Machine.

Weak Spot

Otis Lister grabbed Charley Farley as he walked past. He looked left and looked right, then opened the door to the staff bathroom and pulled Farley inside. He carefully locked the door behind him. "Charley," he hissed. "We need to talk."

"What's up?" asked Mr. Farley, looking around nervously.

"Did you realize that they were having a detention 'party' after school in Mrs. Maxwell's class?"

"A party?"

"Yes. I said something to Raggie this morning, something stern and fatherly, a shame he had to waste his time staying after school and so on. And he told me he had had *fun* in detention! They had a party—the whole class. *Awesome* was the word he used, I think. And they're doing it again tomorrow—all week in fact."

"But—" sputtered Mr. Farley.

"So much for your trust-me-I'm-never-wrong. Never ever wrong! 'Trust me on this, Otis old boy!' Huh! Well, we're in a fine mess. The kids won't drive Mrs. Maxwell

away. And Mr. Bickle won't fire her. What do you suggest now, Mr. I'm Never Wrong?"

Farley had been looking crestfallen, but now he perked up.

"Wait a minute," he said. "We could make this work to our advantage. We'll go over Bickle's head—straight to his boss."

"The school board?"

"Somehow, somehow, we have to make the school board see that Mrs. Maxwell is a dangerous fool, a fruitcake—and that Bickle is an even worse fool for having hired her. Yes, that way we can kill two birds with one stone, get rid of her and Bickle at the same time. You could send the board a memo about Mrs. Maxwell, expressing some of your doubts about her—in the kindest, gentlest terms, of course."

Mr. Lister had recovered from his temper tantrum. He nodded.

"Yes, of course. But will that be enough? Don't they need evidence of what a bad teacher she is? Some proof?" He paced back and forth in the small room, trying to think, the speech he was about to deliver momentarily forgotten. Suddenly Charley smiled.

"I've got it," he said. "The Science Fair."

Mr. Lister looked at him quizzically.

"The Science Fair?"

"Yes," said Farley, and he was laughing now. "Don't you see? Her class is bound to turn in something laughable, embarrassingly awful—they've scrapped Mrs. Biggs's project, with only a few weeks to go until the fair. And anything that class produces is bound to be rotten. By contrast," he added, "my project, I mean my *class*'s project, is brilliant—so brilliant that hers will look even more pathetic by comparison. Trust me on this, Otis. Haven't I told you, I'm always right!" He peered at himself in the mirror, straightened his tie, and smoothed back his hair.

"But how does that help us?"

"Don't you see? All the fifth-grade parents will be at the Science Fair, and it just so happens—"

"—that two of those parents are on the school board!" finished Lister for him, with a laugh. "Brilliant, Charley. And I'll see to it that the superintendent comes, too. All you have to do is win. All right, I like this plan." A small frown furrowed his brow. "Though I'd be a lot happier if I knew for sure what her science project was."

"Yes," said Farley. "You're right." Suddenly he smiled. "Don't worry, Otis. I've got it. They have a weak spot. And I think I know how to make the most of it."

"Do what you need to do, Charley. We can't let anything stand in our way," said Otis. "Not anything. Now I have a speech to give."

A minute after Mr. Farley and Mr. Lister left the bathroom, the door to the second stall opened slowly. A tousled head peered out. Then a slim form opened the bathroom door, looked both ways, and bolted.

Who You Callin' a Fruitcake?

"Listen up," said Jimmy. "Raggie has something important to say."

The whole class was gathered on the playground behind the swings. Jimmy gave Raggie a shove. "Go on. Tell them what you heard."

"They're going to get Mrs. Maxwell fired," said Raggie. "Mr. Lister and Mr. Farley. They say she's a fruitcake."

Well, thought Simon, they got what they wanted. Why aren't they cheering? For that matter, why wasn't *he* cheering? With Aunt Mattie gone, his life would be simple again.

But instead of cheers, a silence settled on the group. Then Ethan pulled his yo-yo out of his pocket. He handed it to Julie.

"Looks like you win," he said. Julie didn't move.

"Sink the Sub," explained Mindy. "Remember? It's been only a week, and she's out of here." She pulled her eraser from her pocket and held it out. Julie stared at the yo-yo and the eraser. Then Jimmy pushed through the kids to stand beside her.

"They can't fire Mrs. Maxwell," he said fiercely. "She's *our* sub. Right?"

Julie looked around at the other kids. "Right," she said slowly. She pushed the yo-yo and the eraser away. "And *no one* calls our sub a fruitcake. No one." She smiled at Jimmy. And then everyone else, Simon included, took up the cry: "Yeah," they shouted. "No one fires our sub but *us*."

Julie turned to Raggie. "Okay, Raggie," she said. "Tell us everything you know."

Permission to Breathe

"It has come to my attention," said Mr. Lister, "that you have been conducting science experiments in your classroom."

"Yes," said Matilda, hurriedly putting Runcible back in her cage and locking her door. Ever since their first encounter, Runcible had taken a strong dislike to Mr. Lister. Parrots can do that. Some people they love at first sight, others they hate. And like elephants, they live a long time and have very long memories. Once a parrot has decided that you are dog meat, it's all over for you. "Behave yourself, you reprobate," Matilda warned.

"I beg your pardon?" asked Mr. Lister, with a deeply offended expression on his face.

"I was addressing the parrot, dear boy."

"Oh. Well, as I said, you are doing science experiments in the classroom." He surveyed the empty room—it was recess time, the children were outside. At the back of the room, the embryonic Egg Machine was covered with a blue plastic tarp, to protect it from pry-

ing eyes. "By the way, what exactly is it that you are doing for the Fair?"

"I'm afraid that's classified as Top Secret," said Matilda. "The children have the strange notion that if word gets out, it may be sabotaged."

"Sabotaged? How absurd! How ridiculous! I merely asked from curiosity. I am sure it is a very fine and laudable—"

"Yes," said Matilda proudly. "It's a humdinger. A lolla-paloosa. They've a good chance for a prize."

Mr. Lister produced a huge sheaf of papers. "Yes, I'm sure," he said with another curious glance in the direction of the tarp. "However, I must ask, have you had the children and their parents sign a consent form?"

"We need their consent to do science experiments?" asked Matilda, incredulous.

"Of course you do. School policy. We could be sued. Here are the papers. No more experiments until every student and every parent has signed one of these and brought it back to the office."

Matilda looked at the paper. "Permission to Conduct Science Experiments. I find this hard to believe."

"Times have changed since you were in school," said Lister flatly. He produced a second batch of papers. "And if you are conducting class after school hours, you will need to have students and their parents—both parents—read and sign these papers as well."

He handed Matilda a batch of three-page sheets entitled Extracurricular Policy and Procedures for Alcohol and Drugs.

"But we are not using alcohol or drugs in our experiment."

"I should hope *not*! But the students need to sign a form saying they will refrain from alcohol or drugs while participating in extracurricular activities."

"I see. Are popcorn and lemonade okay?"

Lister ignored her.

"And these." Another three-page sheet labeled Standards of Behavior for Participating in Extracurricular Activities. "This explains what is and isn't acceptable behavior on school grounds."

"My dear Mr. Lister, I think I can explain that to the students perfectly well."

"We need a signed form. School policy. And these, too." A two-page sheet: Contract for Science Fair Behavior. "That explains that if you cheat on the project you automatically get a zero."

"I should have thought that was obvious. Anything else?"

"Well, that pretty much covers science and extracurricular activities."

"Don't they need to sign a form saying they will not manufacture bombs during science lab?"

"This is not a joking matter," said Lister sternly. "But, now that you mention dangerous experiments, it has come to my attention, via the school nurse, that two children required medical attention as a result of your science experiment."

"Yes, if you consider an ice cube medical attention. Poor things. Two of them seemed to think that the

point of our experiment was to prove that if you hit your thumb with a hammer, it would hurt like the dickens. I applied some ice."

"Again, no joking matter." He produced another sheaf of papers. "You will need to fill out these forms in triplicate for each child who was injured and have them signed by the school nurse and all the parents involved."

Matilda looked at them. School Accident Report Form. "But I sent a note home to their parents explaining what happened."

"Not good enough. Lawsuits, don't you know. Lawsuits. And all the children's parents will have to sign these forms as well. I understand you applied Band-Aids to the two fingers in question?"

"Yes. They didn't really need them, but have you ever

noticed how children seem to find it comforting to have a Band-Aid applied?"

"No, I haven't. And you—"

"Especially if it has dinosaurs or rocket ships on it. These had dinosaurs. Oh, and I gave one child an aspirin."

"Very bad!" said Lister. "Very wrong. Illegal, in fact."

"He had a headache. Oh dear. Must I file a copy of the School Headache Report Form?"

"The problem is, we did not have on file a copy of this"—he produced another piece of paper—"signed by the parent: Permission to Administer Medications."

Matilda smiled at the papers. "Do I need to have them all notarized? Witnessed? Approved by the President?"

"No," said Lister, who did not appear to notice her attempt at humor. "Just the parents. But this separate page, Physician Consent Form, must also be signed by each child's personal doctor. In the future, you may not administer any medications, even aspirin or aspirin substitutes, without a signed copy of both these forms. Is that quite clear?"

Matilda looked at the huge stack of papers he had placed on her desk.

"Whatta loada baloney."

As usual, it was Runcible. Having the last word. Matilda glared at her.

"Runcible, say you're sorry," she said sternly.

Runcible cocked her head and looked straight at Mr. Lister.

"You're sorry," Runcible said. "You're very sorry."

Pecksniffian

"*Rodomontade, rodomontade,*" said Otis Lister, thumbing through the dictionary. He looked up as Charley Farley entered his office.

"Charley. Do you have any idea what *rodomontade* means?"

"No," said Farley. "Funny—I was just going to ask you what *pecksniffian* means. Do you know?"

"No," said Lister. "Why?"

"Well, I caught that pest Raggie in the library without a hall pass, trying to cut *your* assembly—"

"As per usual. Did you give him a warning?"

"You remember what I told you about that class having a weak spot? Well, Raggie's it. I happen to know that Raggie can't afford to get any more detentions. I realized this was my perfect opportunity to pump him about the Science Fair project."

"Good thinking!"

"So I asked him how it was going. 'Just fine,' he says. 'If you tell me about it,' says I, 'perhaps I can give you a little guidance. See if you're headed down a blind alley,

that sort of thing. Save you making mistakes, wasting your time.' "

"Very generous of you, Charley. Very selfless."

"Exactly. Well, that's the sort of person I am. Selfless. Not asking for thanks. But what do you think this wretched boy says to that offer? 'No, thanks,' says he. 'I'm not supposed to discuss the project.' Can you imagine that? And so I decide to give him that warning for not having a hall pass after all, when suddenly Jimmy pops up—I don't know where *he* came from—and says, 'But it was very pecksniffian of you to offer, sir.' 'Yes,' says Raggie. 'Very pecksniffian.' Well, what could I do? I patted him on the head and tore up the warning, then and there."

"Of course. Anyone would have done the same."

"But now I have to look up that word." He reached for the dictionary. "Let me have a quick look. I'm late for lunch duty."

"Sure, here. Funny, it was another one of Mrs. Maxwell's kids who used the word *rodomontade*. I was just going to look it up now. She used it after this morning's assembly. All modesty aside, I thought that was a pretty rousing speech I gave, eh, Charley? About everything I've done for this school. Perhaps I blew my own horn a bit too much. . . ." Here he paused to give Mr. Farley the opportunity to disagree, which Mr. Farley obligingly did.

"Not at all, not at all. We mustn't hide our light under a bushel, my mother always used to say. If we don't sing our own praises, who will?"

"Exactly my line of thought. Bickle would never go

out of his way to sing *my* praises. I doubt he even knows I really exist. The students need to realize how lucky they are to be in a school with an assistant principal who cares about standards and policies and discipline . . ."

"Absolutely. Especially discipline."

"And if there happened to be a few parents and the superintendent of schools in the audience that morning, as luck would have it, well, what harm could it do for them to know the truth about who is the real strength behind this school administration?"

Farley looked up from the dictionary. "Harm? Well, I should think quite the opposite. It's high time they knew what a broken reed Herbert J. Bickle is."

"Yes. A broken reed. Really, completely hopeless, that man. Anyway, afterward that girl, what's her name, Julie. The wise-mouth."

"The one who calls you 'Mr. Listerine' behind your back?"

Otis Lister made a sour face. "The same. Well, she came up to me just now with a big smile and said she thought my speech had been quite a rodomontade. I thanked her."

"Quite right," said Farley.

"I must admit"—here he smiled modestly—"I felt it was quite an accomplishment that a humble little speech of mine could make such a deep impression on a hopeless child like that. It was a good speech, though, wasn't it? You don't think I was overreaching just a little when I said that bit about how the 'flower of our youth must be planted with a firm hand in the garden of—'"

"The devil!" said Farley.

"No, it wasn't the garden of the devil. It was—"

"I mean Raggie. And Jimmy. Those devils. Why, that little wretch!"

"What is it? What's wrong?"

Farley handed the dictionary back to Lister. He pointed to the definition of *pecksniffian*.

"'Selfish and corrupt, behind a false display of good-will,'" read Mr. Lister. "Good lord. What cheek. What erve. You must send him to the principal's office at ice."

"How can I?" sputtered Farley. "I already thanked m for the compliment." He paced angrily back and rth in the cramped office. A sudden thought occurred ɔ him. "You'd better look up rodo-whatever-it-is."

"Rodomontade," said Mr. Lister slowly. A deep red flush was creeping into his cheeks. "I've just found it." Mr. Farley looked over his shoulder, and read aloud:

"'Rodomontade. Vain boasting or bluster. A bragging speech.'"

A silence fell. The two men looked at each other. Finally Mr. Lister slammed the dictionary shut.

"That tears it," he said. "Someone has to teach that class a lesson. They are out of control."

"No one can get away with rudeness like that."

"Somehow, I don't know why, but I suspect Mrs. Maxwell is behind all this. She has no sense of respect for authority. None. Not like Mrs. Biggs did. Now *there* was a woman who knew how to keep kids in line. Did I tell you that Mrs. Maxwell once tried to send *me* to the principal's office?"

"Yes," said Mr. Farley. "Many times."

"We must show her up before she makes a laughing-stock of us."

"The Science Fair," said Farley.

"Yes," said Mr. Lister slowly. "The Science Fair."

The Funny Farm

The Field Trip Permission slips were all in order. The yellow school bus was waiting. The Mighty Muculent Egg Machine was packed up and ready to travel. And Simon's stomach was in a knot.

Miss Frescobaldi saw him in the office, delivering the attendance sheet. "Off on a field trip?" she inquired. "I suppose this is your prize for winning the Math Bee? The day off from school."

"Yes," said Simon. "We're going to visit a working farm."

"Anything to get them out of the classroom," said Miss Frescobaldi to the school secretary, with a knowing look. "The students are so hard to control at this time of year. Summer beckons."

"No," Simon said. "We're field-testing our Science Fair project." I just wish we didn't have to test it at this particular farm, he added to himself. At that moment his class filed by on their way to the bus.

"You're testing the egg machine?" Miss Frescobaldi asked Matilda.

"It's supposed to be a secret," Matilda said to her.

"The children are convinced that someone will try to sabotage it if word gets out what we are making."

Miss Frescobaldi made the gesture of zipping her lips, locking them, and throwing away the key. "Not another word about it," she said. "I wish you the best of luck. Bring me back some farm-fresh eggs."

"Duck or peacock?" asked Matilda.

Miss Frescobaldi laughed. "Peacock, of course."

But Simon knew that Aunt Matilda had been quite serious.

Not long afterward the bus pulled into the dusty driveway of Matilda's farm and came to a stop at the rambling red farmhouse that Simon knew and loved so well. But on this day the sight of the farm filled him with anxiety.

Little had changed since his last visit. There were the peacocks on the roof, still; the motorcycle and bed frame in the yard, still; the dozens of cats lounging in the shade of the front veranda, as always. The daffodils in the flower boxes had been replaced with red geraniums, but they were being eaten, as usual, by Sugar, the sway-backed white horse. In the paddock behind the barn Simon could see Uncle Philbert performing some chore. He, along with the three llamas roaming the paddock, came and leaned against the fence for a closer look at the schoolchildren piling out of the bus.

Scuffing around the dirt in front of the barn was a funny-looking black-and-white-flecked hen that Simon had never seen before. It made an extraordinary

noise—something like a turkey with a bad case of the hiccups.

"I didn't think you had chickens," said Simon to Aunt Mattie.

Julie looked at him with her funny, half-closed-eyes look. "How would you know?" she asked.

"Well," said Simon, flustered, "I mean, they don't seem like the kind of animal Aun—Mrs. Maxwell would have. They're too . . . too useful. None of the other animals are very useful." Julie gave him another Look.

"Simon's right," said Aunt Mattie quickly. "I generally only like animals other people don't want because they aren't useful, or because they've outlived their usefulness. Peacocks, for instance, don't do anything useful, but they are so lovely to look at. Kind of like beautiful flowers that come to life and make ugly noises.

"No, I acquired Henrietta here—and she's actually a guinea hen—because when chickens get to a certain age, they stop laying eggs regularly. Then they get made into chicken stroganoff or something, and that never seemed to me to be a good reward for having spent your life providing breakfast for people.

"Now the funny thing is that, much as I love animals, I can't get them to behave at all. Even Runcible, isn't that right, Runcible?" She addressed the parrot in her cage.

"Get over it," said Runcible with a flap of her wings.

"You see what I mean? I can make any kind of machine work—cars, motorcycles, lawnmowers—but animals, well, I leave that to Uncle Philbert. The ani-

mals love him. Even Henrietta started laying again when he got his hands on her."

It was true. Though Aunt Mattie loved all kinds of animals, and collected and rescued huge numbers of them, on the whole they declined to treat her with the respect she deserved. The stray cats she took in from the cold howled in protest if she should go so far as to tread or sit upon them, as she frequently did. The llamas, far from being grateful to her when she fed them, often rewarded her for her troubles with a nip. The horses, saved from the glue factory, refused, simply refused, to do a single thing she asked of them, planting their feet like mules when she tried to push or pull them in a given direction. Even ducks and chickens scattered at her approach.

But Uncle Philbert—that was another story entirely. The horses gentled under his touch, the llamas became absolutely bashful, the ducks practically ran up to sit in his lap, and the cats purred with contentment whenever he was near.

"Tosh," said Philbert, coming around the corner with a bucket of hen food. "All I did to Henrietta was give her some vitamins and calcium. That's all she needed." He scooped her up and stared her in the face. "And a little encouragement. A pep talk. Right, Henny Penny?"

Aunt Mattie left the class in Uncle Philbert's care while she went indoors. He showed the children around the farmyard. Simon hung back to the rear of the group, and when they approached the llamas he took special care to stay out of sight. The last time he'd been here, during spring vacation, the biggest one, Mr. Ugly, had

taken a strong dislike to him (having something to do with a spitting contest, about which the less said the better). Llamas, like parrots, had long memories and Simon was not anxious for Mr. Ugly to demonstrate that they were old friends—or rather old enemies.

But the llamas—perhaps because of Uncle Philbert's influence—were on their best behavior today. They allowed Mindy and Mandy and Mollie to stroke them, and they didn't seem to mind being told they had beautiful big eyes or lovely eyelashes. Then Philbert introduced the children to a few of the cats. "This one here," he said, undraping a limp white cat from its warm perch on a bale of hay and passing it around, "is Priscilla Goodcat. Most useless varmint ever invented, a complete waste of oxygen. Why, she couldn't catch a mouse if it walked into her mouth and down her throat. And this one"—he picked up a striped tomcat—"is B. Bobbin Badcat. Another waste of cat food. Thinks his job is to be on the wrong side of a door. Yup, never met a door he didn't want to be on the other side of . . ."

Fortunately, Mr. Ugly never caught wind of Simon, and Simon was beginning to relax when somebody said, "Hey, look, there's another horse, out in the pasture. Can we go see him, Mr. Maxwell?"

Uncle Philbert surveyed the group of children. "Even better," he said, "let's call him in. Is there anyone here who can whistle with their fingers?" Silence. Everyone looked at everyone else.

"Tarnation, what's the world comin' to?" asked Uncle Philbert crossly. "What do they teach you in school these days?"

Jimmy turned to Simon. "What about you?" he said. "I thought you said you had just learned to whistle. Your uncle taught you or something."

"Yuh, okay," muttered Simon. "It's just I'm not very good." But he placed his fingers to his mouth and gave a short, extremely good, whistle. As Simon had known he would, the chestnut horse at the far end of the pasture jerked his head up, listened a second, and cantered over to them. The moment Hero—for that was his name—saw Simon, he whinnied, stuck his head over the fence, nuzzled Simon's chest with his head, and began nibbling at his shirt pockets.

"Hey, stop that," said Simon, blushing.

"Wow," said Julie. "You'd think he knew you or something. What's he doing?"

"I believe," said Uncle Philbert, pulling some carrots out of his pocket, "he's looking for these." He passed the carrots out among the students, being sure to press several extra ones into Simon's hand.

Julie looked right at Simon. "You *sure* he doesn't know you?" she asked.

At that moment Aunt Mattie returned, puffing and extremely red-faced. "I can't catch that blasted hen for the life of me," she said. "She won't hold still for one second."

"Now why do you want to do that?" asked Philbert.

"We have to try out our Egg Machine," said Mattie. "It's time to stop playing and get down to work."

"You're right. It's time for some lessons," said Philbert. "This is supposed to be an educational field trip, ain't it? All play and no work makes Jack a dull boy

128

and Jill a dull girl. For starters it is impossible to chase animals without first learning to whistle." So he administered lessons in whistling with your fingers. After twenty minutes, there were a large number of very dizzy children, and a small number who could make some faint, watery whistling noises through their fingers. After that he taught the children how to make owl and whippoorwill calls by blowing into their cupped hands. And having done that, he said it was only natural that they brush up on their ability to make duck calls using a blade of grass between their thumbs.

Once they were done with these lessons he announced that it was time to scientifically test the principles of skipping stones on the duck pond. To his horror, there were children who did not know how to skip stones.

"What's the world comin' to?" he asked again peevishly. "Now look here, you young whiffet. What's your name?"

"Julie."

"You throw a stone like that, it's not gonna skip. It's gonna sink like a, like a—"

"Like a stone?" offered Julie.

"Yep, like a stone. Now, you gotta cock your arm like this."

Julie gave it another try. Uncle Philbert looked disgusted.

"Did anyone ever tell you you throw like a girl?"

Julie looked at him coolly. "I am a girl," she said. Simon grinned. Uncle Philbert, well known to be one of the rudest men on earth, might have met his match.

"Nothin' we can do about that unfortunate fact," said Philbert calmly. "But just mebbe we can teach you to skip stones."

Within fifteen minutes, all the children in the class had mastered the scientific principles of skipping stones. Even Julie got one to skip a half-dozen times. Then Uncle Philbert called a halt and announced that it was time to scientifically test the temperature of the water in the pond.

And so the Egg Machine was forgotten while the children changed into bathing suits and spent the rest of the morning chasing ducks, getting muddy, swimming, getting muddy, and swimming. Afterward they ate lunch on the veranda.

When the last lunch box had been put away, Aunt Mattie said, "Now, can we catch that miserable hen?"

"You leave that to me, Mattie," said Philbert. And he hitched up his pants, strode off to the barnyard, and returned in five minutes with the guinea hen tucked under his arm, gurgling contentedly. (The hen, that is, not Philbert.)

"I declare, you are a magician with animals, Bertie. I must have chased that foolish fowl for fifteen minutes."

"You stick to machines," said Philbert, "and leave the animals to me." He patted the hen on the head. "Ain't that right, Henny Penny? Now where's this infernal contraption?"

The infernal contraption, as Philbert was to refer to it henceforward, had been set up on the back porch. With

the guinea hen still tucked under his arm, Philbert walked all around it, peering suspiciously.

"I don't trust it," he said. "Doesn't look safe."

He reached out his free hand to touch it.

"No!" shouted Simon, and immediately got flustered. Everyone turned to look at him. "I mean, I mean—"

"The boy's quite right," said Aunt Mattie, jumping to his aid. "Keep your cotton-pickin' hands off it." She turned to the startled class to explain what Simon already knew. "Mr. Maxwell may be good with animals, but he is death to machines. Death. One touch and it's all over. *Finito*. Kaput. Sayonara."

Simon knew from personal experience that she was not exaggerating. He had seen Uncle Philbert destroy machines ranging from toasters to one-ton farm tractors. Sometimes, it seemed, he just had to look at them sideways for them to fall apart. Why, the dishwasher in Mattie's kitchen had been put permanently out of order by a single well-meaning attempt on Philbert's part to clean out the filter. (The next time they had run it, the plates and cups had emerged as thousands of small fragments of glass and china. It was now used as Mattie's desk and bookshelf.) On another occasion Simon had personally witnessed Philbert disable a sports car by simply laying his hands on the hood of the car. Fried the solenoid, just like that.

"Well," said Philbert, with a hurt look, "no need to be rude, you know. I was only tryin' to help."

"Well, dear, why don't you limit yourself to convincing Henrietta to lay an egg so we can try out our contraption here? It's all plugged in and ready to go."

"I don't know," said Philbert, stroking Henrietta's head. "She's quite unpredictable."

But he put her in the nest box at the top of the Egg Machine, bent over, and murmured a few words in her ear. Henrietta responded by ruffling up her feathers,

making a few happy hiccuping sounds, and settling herself down into the straw.

"Cluck," she said, quite clearly, and then cocked her head to one side, looking at Philbert with her beady bright eyes.

"Go ahead," said Philbert. "Turn it on. She's ready. Or as ready as she'll ever be."

So they turned it on. There were, of course, a few bugs that needed working out. Once, when it seemed they were finally about to get it running, Uncle Philbert insisted on helping out by tightening a small screw. The "infernal contraption" instantly stopped and had to be completely recalibrated. After a few of these trial runs—or, rather, trial-and-error runs—everything and everyone got thoroughly covered in egg yolk, egg white, and scrambled egg. But they got back on the bus two hours later, tired and happy, if a bit, well, muculent.

Just Too Weird?

CLUCK

The Science Fair was held in the giant gymnasium of a local high school. Twenty fifth grades from seven schools around the county were there. The place was crammed with people looking frightfully busy and frightfully scientific. There were students and teachers, parents and principals, judges and onlookers.

They had been there bright and early setting up displays explaining the principles of composting and computing, photosynthesis and photography, geography and geology, the life cycle of plants, the social system of ants, fossils and missiles, water pollution, the moon's revolutions around the earth, the earth's revolutions around the sun, meal worm digestion and traffic congestion, and much much more. All of which Simon had seen in one form or another at every science fair he had ever been to.

The only thing that wasn't there was the Mighty Muculent Egg Machine. Simon was not worried about that—Aunt Mattie was always late. What did worry him, though, more and more as he wandered up and

down the aisles looking at the other exhibits, was that none of the displays remotely resembled his class's project. Trust his class and Aunt Mattie to come up with something that no one had ever done before. Would everyone make fun of the Egg Machine? Would they be a laughingstock? Why had nobody stood up and said, "Hey, this is just too weird"? Because no one had ever stopped to think about it, that's why. Because everyone—even diehards like Julie and Jimmy—had been having too much fun doing it. But now it was Truth Time. And Truth Time looked like it might be painful.

Suddenly Simon stopped. He had come to the exhibit of Mr. Farley's class. At least fifty students were clustered around a big, professional-looking three-sided display. The printing on the board had been done in large, sophisticated type with computer-generated color graphics. It read:

Working Home Computer
It adds! It subtracts! It divides! It multiplies!
Constructed by
Mr. Charles Farley's Fifth Grade
(Defending State Champions)
Check it out!!!

Simon pushed through the kids waiting to try the computer. On the table was a plain, crude computer with a keyboard (very like one Simon had seen at Pflummerfield Electronics the other day) and a single logic board open for viewing. It was hooked up to a television screen, instead of a monitor—to make it look

more homemade, Simon guessed. But surely the judges wouldn't be fooled. Would they?

Simon stood around for a while, watching the other kids use the computer, listening to their comments. "Awesome" was the one he heard most often, followed by "You guys really made this yourselves?" and "You're gonna win first prize for sure."

Suddenly he heard a commotion by the entry to the gym. It was Aunt Mattie and Uncle Philbert, making their way through the crowd, followed by a number of students lugging heavy cardboard boxes containing the disassembled Egg Machine. Much of the commotion was caused by Runcible, who was sidestepping up and down Mattie's shoulder, squawking, whistling, flapping her wings, and calling out loudly, "Heave-ho, mateys! Heave-ho! Wrawk. Outta my way, dog breath. Make a lane there. Make a lane."

"Oh, you jackanape!" cried Mattie, as Runcible's

claws dug into her neck. "Hold still. That hurts, you miserable miscreant."

"Thank you," said Runcible. "Please. Say thank you. Say please."

"Come to Papa," said Uncle Philbert, taking the parrot, who immediately calmed down and began nibbling his ear. "Mebbe you should've left her at home."

"The children wouldn't let me. They say she's their mascot."

"Do you hear that, Runcible?" said Philbert. "You're the class mascot. Now, you gotta make us proud of you."

Runcible, who was clearly feeling very nautical—not to mention naughty—stood at attention on Philbert's shoulder and suddenly began singing snatches of a sea chantey that was so rude it would have made even a sailor blush.

"Heave-ho, haul away for Rosie-o," she began in a surprisingly good voice. "Behind the pub with her—"

But evidently even Philbert had had enough. He plucked the parrot from his shoulder, and as soon as they got to their booth he deposited her in the cage. This he put under the table, next to the cardboard cat-carrying box that held Henrietta the guinea hen. "Perhaps you can teach Runcible some manners, Henny," he said.

The crowd around Simon had gradually become aware of the commotion surrounding the new arrivals, and they turned from the computer display to watch. "What a circus," said one parent. "Whose class is that?"

"It's Mrs. Maxwell and her Mighty Muculent Men," said Wilton Pflummerfield, and the kids around him snickered. Simon was reminded of Julie's Parallel Universe theory. Here it was all over again. Somehow Aunt Mattie had worked her magic on them, made them all think her brand of lunacy, their science project, their Egg Machine, was fine and possible, a winner even. But now, exposed to the harsh light of the everyday world—the Real Universe—it appeared ridiculous, absurd, embarrassing. How could this be?

"Why are you looking so gloomy?" said a voice beside him. It was Julie. Simon didn't answer right away.

"I was thinking about the Egg Machine," he said at last. "We're going to get laughed right out of the Science Fair, aren't we?"

"Hey," said Julie, "have you forgotten that it stars the great Julie Biedermeyer?" She made a grandiose gesture, and Simon managed a grin.

"Maybe that's exactly what I meant," he said. Julie laughed, and then turned serious.

"So maybe we will get laughed at," she said. "So who cares?" She gave him a funny look. "Maybe sometimes you just have to believe in something, no matter how weird it looks to other people, you know?"

Simon stared at her. "What do you mean?"

But before she could answer, Mindy showed up, saying they had to get the display set up. They hurried over to their table. Instantly, Mr. Lister appeared, with a clipboard in his hand.

"You're late," he said. "You were supposed to have been all set up by now. The judging starts soon."

"That's good," said Matilda. "Being late adds to the suspense, don't you think? Everyone must be asking themselves, Where oh where is the Mighty Egg Machine?"

"This is not a drama contest, Mrs. Maxwell. It is a Science Fair." Mr. Lister pressed his lips together and glanced down at his clipboard. "You are scheduled to give your presentation in fifty-five minutes. If you are late for *that,* you are disqualified. Dis-qual-i-fied," he repeated.

Each class had just ten minutes to explain their project to the judges and demonstrate how it worked. All morning the judges and other students had had a chance to cruise around looking at all the displays. But the actual demonstration was crucial—especially for the Mighty Muculent Egg-Breaking and Breakfast-Making Morning-Waking Machine, since it could actually function only once, using an egg from Henrietta. The rest of

the time, it had to just sit there. For this reason, the class had decided to keep the machine hidden behind a curtain until the moment of the demonstration. To add to the suspense. All there was to see at this point was a large poster, hand drawn by Sebastian, with text by Mindy. Yesterday Simon had thought it was brilliant. Today, compared to Mr. Farley's display, it looked babyish and crude.

While Matilda's class was setting up, Mr. Farley and several of his students came by to watch.

"May I help in any little way?" offered Mr. Farley, gazing curiously at the poster. Simon noticed Wilton Pflummerfield trying to see behind the curtain. "I realize you are a little behind schedule, and we have some time to spare."

"The children feel particularly strongly that they must do every aspect of the project without grown-up help. Even I am not allowed to assist," said Matilda. "That way they can really say it is their own work, however flawed. I'm sure you understand."

Mr. Farley flushed but kept his smile in place. "Sure," he said. "Very honorable. My students have the same policy. The same. Don't we, kids?" The students, who'd been busily examining the booth area, looked up.

"Hunh?" said Wilton. "Oh, um, yeah. Yeah. We worked real hard on our project, and we're going to kick butt."

"Yes?" said Mrs. Maxwell kindly. "Go on. You're going to kick, but what?"

"No, I meant, kick, you know, kick . . ." Suddenly he got flustered and couldn't finish his sentence.

"So," said Mr. Farley, looking at the poster. "It's a Mighty Muculent Egg-Breaking and Breakfast-Making Morning-Waking Machine, eh, 'featuring Henrietta the Heroic Hen'? Sounds more like a science-fiction movie than a science project."

"It's a little of everything, actually," said Mattie.

"What on earth *is* it? And more to the point, what scientific principles does it demonstrate?"

"Goodness, I suppose it shows that when children put their minds to something, they can—"

"Cluck!"

"Cluck?" Mr. Farley bent over and looked under the table. Henrietta poked her head through a hole in the cat box. "Cluck!" she repeated. From her cage next door, Runcible gave the hen a dirty look and said, "Shut up. Say thank you. Get a life."

Mr. Farley straightened up, a condescending smile on his lips. The other students were clearly trying to keep themselves from laughing.

"This I've got to see," said Mr. Farley.

"Come back at 1:15 and you will," said Matilda tartly.

"I wouldn't miss it for the world," he said, and laughed.

"I agree," said a man who had been listening to the conversation. "I wouldn't miss it for the world, either."

The strange man stepped forward toward the booth, and Simon saw for the first time that he wore a blue ribbon on his lapel, labeled JUDGE.

The smile faded from Mr. Farley's face. He quickly arranged his features into an expression of sincere respect and held out his hand.

"Very pleased to meet you," he said quickly, pumping

the man's hand. "Charles Farley. I do so hope you'll have a chance to stop by our booth, too, before the presentations start."

The judge peered at Mr. Farley's name tag.

"Farley, eh? That's right. The computer, isn't it?"

Mr. Farley's face lit up. "Yes, that's us. Last year's state champions."

"A very impressive display. Very." Farley allowed himself a modest simper and was about to speak when the judge added, "And the kids did it all themselves, did they?"

"Oh, yes, sir," said Wilton Pflummerfield. "We did. All of it. Ourselves."

"Even the gigabyte interface?"

"Uh, sure," said Wilton. "Even the, um, the giggly-bit thing, right, Ralph?"

"Yeah," said Ralph. "The giggly-bit part was easy."

The judge nodded thoughtfully. "I found the computer very impressive, as I said. Perhaps the most impressive display I'd seen." Mr. Farley started to say something about how hard the class had worked on it, when he noticed the judge's attention wandering. He was looking again at the poster of the Egg Machine.

"But now *this*," said the judge, "*this* is something I've never seen before."

Julie dug her elbow into Simon's ribs. "Hey!" she whispered. "He likes it."

Much as Simon wanted to believe her, he was only too aware that the judge's comment could be taken two entirely different ways.

Ace in the Hole

"I can't believe it," said Otis Lister, pacing up and down in the auditorium hallway. "Is it really possible that that old woman and those, those ignoramus students can have made something that will win the Science Fair?"

"It seems impossible," said Mr. Farley. "But—"

"I wrote every member of the school board and informed them about the problem with Mrs. Maxwell and Bickle's refusal to fire her. Then I invited them all to the Science Fair and told them how you would bring honor to the school by winning it, hands down. They're expecting you to win, Charley. If *she* wins, we both look like fools. And Mr. Bickle's job is secure for another year."

"You have to stop her," said Farley.

"Correction," said Mr. Lister. "*We* have to stop her. I have an ace in the hole." He pulled a piece of paper out of his coat pocket. "I was hoping I wouldn't need to use it. But just in case it doesn't work, I need you to do what you can. *Whatever* you can. Do you catch my drift?"

"Yes," said Farley grimly. "Yes, I catch your drift."

"Good. Now please tell Mrs. Maxwell that I need to speak to her urgently."

Mr. Lister met Matilda outdoors by the teeter-totters. Mattie did not arrive promptly, of course, and Mr. Lister was fidgeting nervously by the time she did arrive.

"What is it, dear?" asked Mrs. Maxwell. "Where's the fire?"

"No fire," said Mr. Lister, pulling the paper slowly from his coat. "I just need to ask you—"

"Of course," said Mattie. "Ask away."

"I need you—"

"Excuse me," said Mattie. "But your shoelace is untied. So dangerous, an untied lace."

Mr. Lister flushed and tied his shoe. He stood up. He straightened his tie. He cleared his throat. At last he spoke. "You must withdraw your entry in the Science Fair."

Matilda was flabbergasted. "Why should I do that?"

"It has come to my attention that you have not completed the necessary paperwork—permission forms and so on. You will remember I gave them to you some time ago. If the judges find out, which they will, you must be disqualified."

Matilda broke into a smile. "Oh, if that's all," she said. Then she bent over her enormous purse and began to empty its contents onto the ground. Out came a fold-up umbrella, one left shoe, a telephone book for Schenectady, New York, a bag of carrots, a bag of parrot food, two screwdrivers (regular and Phillips head), a bag of

144

porcupine quills, a bag of feathers, a back scratcher, Band-Aids, butterscotch candy, and finally a bulging manila folder. She removed a handful of papers.

"Here they are," she said, thrusting them at Mr. Lister. "Contract for Science Fair Behavior." He looked at them, unsmiling, and read each one carefully.

"Yes. They appear to be all here." He gave her a thin smile. "However, I still must insist that you withdraw your entry. You needn't concern yourself with the reason."

Matilda stared at him. "Why would I do that?"

"If you wish to keep your job. You see, Mrs. Maxwell, you do things in a most unorthodox manner. That may work on a farm, but in a school, we must do things in the correct and orderly way. Chaos has no place in a school. We have policies and rules, and you have broken almost every rule I can think of." He read from the paper he was holding. "Administering medicine without a consent form—"

"An aspirin?"

"Quite illegal, as I told you. Then this matter of bringing animals into the classroom—"

"Runcible?"

"The school board has a firm policy on that. Putting student lives in danger, you know."

"A life-threatening parrot?"

"Allergies, Mrs. Maxwell. Allergies are no laughing matter. Therefore, a strict no-pets policy."

"But Runcible is not a pet. She was part of a science experiment: the feather and the quill. Besides, no one in the class has parrot allergies."

"Nonetheless, the school policy is quite clear."

Matilda sighed. She pulled out the folder again and handed the whole thing to Mr. Lister.

"What's all this, then?" he asked, shuffling through the mass of paperwork. "What on earth is all this?"

"Papers. Forms. Permission slips. What-have-you. I think you'll find it's all there, as requested. Plus a few others I threw in myself, just to be on the safe side."

Mr. Lister picked up a sheet at random. "What's this? I never requested this. Permission to Administer Spelling Test? And this? Consent Form for Vocabulary

Lessons? Extracurricular Policy for Cookies and Lemonade?"

"Yes, many of the parents were dismayed by all the paperwork, but I assured them that this was the way Mr. Lister liked things done. I think you'll find the aspirin forms are there as well. And all the others you wanted."

"They had better be complete. If just one is missing, it is enough to get you fired. And just between you and I, it is quite easy to fire substitutes. I'm giving you one last—"

" 'You and *me*.' "

"Hunh?"

" 'Just between you and *me*.' Grammar, Mr. Lister." Matilda looked down at her hands for a minute. "I would be sad to leave my students," she said. "I have enjoyed them very much."

"Are you telling me that you will not withdraw your entry?"

"I can't, Mr. Lister. Even if I wanted to. It's not really *my* entry. It is entirely the children's. They thought it up. They made it."

"Then Monday could be your last day here, you understand that?"

"If that's the way it has to be. Good day, Mr. Lister."

"Think it over, Mrs. Maxwell," he called after her. "You have half an hour to change your mind."

Fowl Play

batteries ✓
music ✓
remote control ✓
guinea pig ✓
guinea hen ✓

Where was Aunt Mattie? Simon glanced at the clock over the door. It was the same kind of round, white clock you saw in every gymnasium you went into. It said 12:40. Twenty minutes to one. Only thirty-five minutes until the time to present to the judges.

Nor was Uncle Philbert anywhere to be seen. He had been dispatched to find an extra extension cord (really it was just an excuse to keep him away from the Egg Machine). And a kind of controlled pandemonium was in progress at the class's booth. Mindy and Mandy were going over final changes in the speech they had written for the presentation. Julie, who was to read the speech, was walking up and down practicing it, accompanying it with many dramatic hand gestures. Mollie was checking batteries. And other students were adding the last touches to the poster or to the Egg Machine itself. After the judge made his comments, a kind of panicky hope had filled the students—the possibility, the actual possibility that they might win the Science Fair. Even Simon, against his better judgment, found himself catching the excitement. Who knows, he thought. Ever

since Aunt Mattie with her outlandish ways had blown into his life, everything he had ever taken for granted had been turned upside down. Maybe this would be, too.

"Listen," said Sebastian, once everything had been assembled. "Let's run through the checklist, to be sure we're all ready to go. It's getting late."

"But Aunt—Mrs. Maxwell's not back," said Simon. Where *was* she?

"We don't need her," said Julie. "And I know she'd agree." The students began to run through the list: Batteries? Check. Music? Check. Remote control? Check. Guinea pig? Check. Guinea hen?

No answer.

"Guinea hen? Raggie?"

There was a shout from under the table. It was Raggie. He stood up and looked around in panic.

"What is it?" asked Mindy.

"It's Henrietta," Raggie said. "She's gone."

Sabotage

"What do you mean, gone? Did she escape from the box? Come on, we can find her," said Mindy.

"No," said Raggie. "Really gone. The whole box and everything. Someone must've took her."

Total silence fell as the students realized the extent of the disaster. No hen. No eggs. Therefore no Egg Machine. Finally Raggie said what everyone was thinking.

"Sabotage."

The students all began talking at once.

"I knew it!"

"Yeah, it's those creeps from Mr. Farley's class. I saw them messing around behind the table about fifteen minutes ago. They'd do anything to win—even cheat."

"They kidnapped our hen!"

"What'll we do?"

"Shouldn't we wait for Mrs. Maxwell?" asked Simon.

"There isn't time," said Jimmy. "Let's go get Henny back!"

"Wait a minute," said Simon. "Raggie, you run over to Mr. Farley's booth and ask if anyone has seen

Henrietta. Maybe someone picked up her box by mistake."

"Yeah," muttered Mario under his breath. "Like they mistook her for a box of Chicken Nuggets."

Raggie was back in two minutes. "They all say they haven't seen her," he panted. He didn't add that any three-year-old could have told that they were lying.

"Sure," said Julie. "What did you expect?" Everyone nodded, and an angry, glum silence descended.

"What're we gonna do?" moaned Mindy.

"All this work, and for nothing," said Jimmy. He kicked a table leg. "I say we all march over there together, right now, and demand that they give Henrietta back. Tell them we'll smash their computer if they don't."

There was a chorus of agreement. Jimmy picked up a hammer. So did Ethan. "Let's go!" they said.

"Wait!" said Simon, looking around desperately for his aunt. "This isn't what Mrs. Maxwell would want us to do."

"How do you know what she would want?" growled Jimmy. He was still clutching his hammer.

"I just do," said Simon.

"Simon's right," said Julie. "Mrs. Maxwell would say something like"—and she put on her best, crisp Aunt Mattie voice—"'You know very well that violence solves nothing.'"

Her imitation of Aunt Mattie was so convincing that a collective sigh of disappointment ran through the class. Jimmy put down his hammer. So did Ethan.

There was another long silence. Simon looked at the clock. It was ten to one. Time was running out. Then Raggie stepped forward.

"Violence isn't right," said little Raggie, and Simon wanted to shake his hand. Then he went on. "But there's another way to sabotage it—a nonviolent way. And they'll never guess we did it."

"How?"

Raggie looked around at the group with his crooked grin. "We have a secret weapon," he said.

Everyone looked at him blankly. Just then Philbert showed up at a trot, out of breath and clutching a bright orange extension cord.

"I found a cord," he announced. "But danged if I can get it to work."

Her What?

CLUCK!

"What?" said Philbert, looking around. "What is it? Why is everyone staring at me? Don't you know it's rude to stare? It's not my fault the danged cord won't work. The janitor told me—"

"Oh, we don't need that cord, Mr. Maxwell," said Julie, stepping forward. "Here, let me have it." She dropped it onto a table. "But we were just kind of wondering if, um, if you had ever used a computer before. Wouldn't you like to try out a computer? Mr. Farley's class has this really neat one at their booth."

"Yeah," chimed in Jimmy. "It's really cool."

"Me?" said Philbert. "Now what use would I have for a computer? I hate the dang things. I can add and subtract perfectly well with a pencil, thank you very much. No, I—"

"Please," said Julie, giving him her most winning smile. "Right now. You have to hurry, because in a few minutes it will be too late."

The class had closed in around Philbert and were slowly propelling him down the gymnasium toward

Mr. Farley's booth, talking quickly as they went. Simon knew what they were up to. All it would take would be a few seconds, just long enough for Uncle Philbert to lay his hands on the computer. Heck, probably all he had to do was look at it and the logic boards would go up in smoke. Simon glanced again at the clock: 12:55. In five minutes, Mr. Farley's class would be giving their presentation to the judges, and it would be too late. Already a small crowd had begun to gather in front of Mr. Farley's booth to view the presentation. He hated to do this, but he had to.

"Stop!"

The lynch mob, if you can call a group of computer slayers a lynch mob, turned and stared at Simon. Simon pushed his way to the front and pulled Philbert away from the mob. "Uncle Philbert," he whispered urgently into his ear, "I need you to go get Aunt Mattie. Right away." Philbert stared. He wasn't used to being issued orders by young whippersnappers, but something in Simon's tone convinced him. He nodded and, with a backward glance at the class, vanished to search for his wife.

"Why'd you do that?" yelled Jimmy angrily. "He was about to do what we wanted."

"Shut up, Jimmy," said Simon. "You know—everyone here knows—it would have been wrong—just as wrong as smashing it with a hammer. Mrs. Maxwell would never have let us get away with that, ever."

Jimmy was still angry. Simon could practically see him forming the thought—Goody-goody!—in his mind. "Yeah," Jimmy taunted him, "so who made you the

154

instant expert on what Mrs. Maxwell thinks? Are you her special pet or something?"

"No," said Simon. He glanced over the faces of the members of his class. Then he took a deep breath and said, "I'm her nephew." This news was greeted with silent stupefaction by all but Julie. Julie shook her head and started laughing.

"Her what?" said Jimmy at last.

"Her great-nephew, actually," said Simon. "And as her great-nephew, I can promise you that if you don't stop trying to sabotage Mr. Farley's class, she'll . . . she'll *gashiate* your *corporosity* when she gets back. So let's find another plan."

There was no time for anyone to discuss Simon's amazing revelation, for it was only too clear that he was right. They had to quickly find another solution. Then, just when things looked the bleakest, Aunt Mattie finally showed up, out of breath, trailing Uncle Philbert. She had a funny look on her face, a look Simon had never seen before. A look that he could only describe as fierce.

As the students filled her in on the disaster, she shook her head several times. But all she said was, "Well, what do you think we should do now? Time's a-wasting."

There was a long and painful silence. At last Mollie raised her hand.

"I guess maybe we could run to a store or something and try to buy some eggs," she said, without a lot of enthusiasm.

"Now you're thinking," said Matilda. But her words were greeted with a gloomy silence.

"Store eggs are boring," said Mindy. "Henrietta's eggs were so nice and round."

"Besides, there isn't time," said Mario. "If we're even a minute late, we get disqualified."

"Never mind," said Matilda. "That's not what's important. Perhaps we won't be allowed to win a ribbon, but I'm sure the judges will still let us do our presentation, and that's what counts. Winning would be gratifying, I'm sure, but the main thing is to show them what we can do. The main thing is the Mighty Muculent Egg Machine. And unless anyone has any other ideas, that's what we'll do. Now, whose parents could go fetch some eggs for us?" A dozen hands were glumly raised.

Raggie looked at Jimmy in surprise. "Your family is here?" he asked. "I thought they only went to basketball recitals, or whatever they're called."

"Yeah, well, that's because I promised them we were going to win."

"Winning isn't everything," continued Matilda. "As my old granny used to say—"

But what her old granny used to say will remain forever a mystery, for it was at that exact moment that Runcible chose to join the discussion.

"Cluck," she said from her cage under the table. "Cluck. Cluck. Cluck."

Runcible to the Rescue

Cluck?

Simon looked at Jimmy. Jimmy looked at Raggie. In fact, everyone looked at everyone else with an expression that the poet Keats would undoubtedly have described as "wild surmise," rather like Cortez's men did when they stood silent on that peak in Darien and for the first time cast their eyes upon the noble Pacific Ocean.

Unlike Cortez's men, however, Simon and his classmates did not stand silent, not for long anyway.

"Runcible!" they clamored. "Runcible! Mrs. Maxwell, do parrots lay eggs? Do they? Is Runcible a girl or a boy? Could she lay an egg? Has she ever laid an egg?"

Matilda looked at Philbert.

"Once," he said. "In 1973. It was a lovely green egg, too. Kinda small. I convinced her not to try again, though. They can't hatch, you see."

"Could she lay an egg for us today, though?"

Philbert stroked his long silver mustache thoughtfully.

"Not likely," he said. "Would take a miracle. Unless

maybe Henrietta has been giving her lessons. Who knows? How much time do we have?"

"About twenty minutes. More, if we can stall."

"Well, no harm tryin'. I'll go have a word with her."

And so Philbert put Runcible in the nesting box that perched atop the Egg Machine and sat down to have a long talk with her, while overhead the hands of the clock crept closer and closer to 1:15.

Cabotinage

At precisely 1:15, the judges headed for the Mighty Muculent Egg Machine exhibit. Behind them were students, and behind them, parents, teachers, and other curious onlookers. They were talking eagerly to each other, but not about the Egg Machine. No, they were talking about Mr. Farley's computer demonstration, which they had just witnessed. Simon's few glimmers of hope were instantly replaced with gloom. All he could hear were comments about how astonishing, how clever, kids these days, isn't it amazing, imagine building a *real computer*. The only one not exclaiming about the computer was the judge who'd stopped by their booth earlier. Simon stared at him, trying hard to believe that the expression on his face was one of disbelief and skepticism. It *could* be. On the other hand—and this is what Simon feared was true—it could also be disbelief and *amazement*.

At last the judges formed a ring around the Egg Machine, and one gave the signal to commence. Mindy stood up.

"We would like to introduce the Mighty Muculent Egg-Breaking and Breakfast-Making Morning-Waking Machine," she began, but she was instantly interrupted by a judge.

"Excuse me," he said. "I don't wish to appear ignorant, but perhaps you could tell us what muculent means?"

"Oh, sure. It means like slimy. We could've said slimy, I guess, but muculent sounded better."

"Quite right," said the judge, and others nodded their heads in agreement. "Proceed."

"Okay." She gave a nervous look over at the Egg Machine. All that was visible of it behind the curtain was Uncle Philbert's head and Runcible, sitting in her nest box, uncharacteristically silent. Philbert was talking to her. The store eggs had not shown up yet. "First I'd like to explain that usually we have a guinea hen here but due to nefarious—"

But Matilda was shaking her head at her and whispering, "No excuses."

"—um, nefarious circumstances beyond our control, we are using a parrot. And we hope it works." She looked back at her notes. "We decided to invent the Egg Machine because nobody, at least none of us, likes to get up in the morning and have to make breakfast feeling all sleepy. So the Egg Machine lets you sleep in while your breakfast is made for you, and then it wakes you up nicely. And your breakfast is all done. It's kind of fun. And we all worked on it, together, each person did. Just us. No grown-ups."

Simon saw the judges smiling and nodding in agree-

ment. He knew that Mindy was playing for time, but the judges didn't seem to care. Mindy looked at the gymnasium door. Still no sign of the store eggs. How much longer could she stall?

"I definitely need one of those," said one judge to another.

"We decided to use a guinea hen because it was kind of inspired by that Dr. Seuss book, *Scrambled Eggs Super*, and it seemed more interesting than regular eggs. I really love that book, don't you?" Mindy was just making stuff up now. She glanced again at the gymnasium door.

"Very literary," said another judge. Several judges laughed, but Simon saw another one frown and look at her watch.

"We need to proceed," she said. "We have many more presentations to hear."

"Right," said Mindy. "Well, we all came up with some stuff and then we built it all by ourselves from plans, and here it is," she finished hurriedly and lamely. "And Julie will explain how it works."

Julie stood up and, using a wooden pointer, gestured toward the hidden Egg Machine.

"Ladies and gentlemen," she said dramatically, talking in the sing-song voice of a carnival showman, "let me introduce to you the one, the only, Mighty Muculent Egg-Breaking and Breakfast-Making Morning-Waking Machine!"

She nodded to Bix and Ethan, who pulled the ropes and opened the curtain that had screened the Egg Machine from view. There it stood, a strange Rube

Goldberg contraption topped with a nest box, in which Runcible the parrot sat looking self-important. Some yards behind it, lying on a table and snoring loudly, was Mario, pretending to be fast asleep.

The crowd laughed, and at that precise instant, Runcible gave a loud squawk, ruffled her wings, and said, unmistakably, "Cluck!" She stood up, sat down, and looked around with a proud and somewhat startled expression in her eyes. Somewhat like those men on the peak in Darien.

Philbert bent over the nest box, stood up, and flashed Julie a huge grin, his thumb and finger making the okay sign. A vast sigh of relief escaped from all of Matilda's students, as well as some cheers and clapping. Simon cheered louder than anyone. Runcible had come through. Great-uncle Philbert and good old Runcible had come through.

"You go, girl!" said Julie happily, and then she seemed to recollect where she was. She put on her serious face. "Yes, the Mighty Egg Machine: It shakes, it bakes, *and* it wakes you up! And at the same time it demonstrates how science can make our lives better, using only the forces of nature—gravity, heat, jet propulsion, laser beams, and shall we say *alternative* forms of energy.

"We start with, as Mindy explained, the simple guinea hen, Latin name *Numida meleagris*." She looked up from her note cards. "Or, uh, in this case the parrot. Latin name, um, *Parrotosis thingummi*." The judges laughed again. Good, thought Simon. Go, Julie.

"Each morning, or perhaps during the night, the hen

will lay an egg in the nest box." She pointed to the nest box with the pointer. "The egg remains in the box until, at a preset time, this nasty alarm clock goes off, startling the hen so that she jumps out of the nest box."

Just then a loud buzzing erupted under the nest box, and Runcible jumped squawking onto Philbert's shoulder.

"Oh, my sainted aunt!" said the parrot. "Shut up!"

Julie continued, trying not to laugh. "The change in weight releases a spring on a trapdoor in the bottom of the nest box, allowing the egg to roll out down this ramp made of Lego pieces"—and indeed, as she spoke, a small green egg could be seen rolling lopsidedly down the ramp. All the students cheered—they couldn't help themselves—at the sight of that lovely little egg.

"Way to go, Runcible!"

CLUCK!

The Mighty Muculent
Egg-Breaking and
Breakfast-Making
Morning-Waking Machine!

Julie resumed.

"The egg shoots off the end of the ramp, into the little basketball hoop, and lands in this strainer." As the egg shot off the ramp and passed perfectly through the small hoop, a voice from the crowd yelled, "Yo! A three-pointer!" Turning, Simon saw a boy in a high-school varsity jacket, who looked like a taller, older version of Jimmy, giving Jimmy a high five. Jimmy was blushing with pleasure.

"Well," continued Julie, "the strainer is really just a metal bowl we punched holes in. Of course, the egg gets smashed to smithereens, and all the egg stuff drips through the strainer, leaving the shells behind."

"Very clever," said one of the judges, and the grown-ups all applauded as the egg did just that.

"Now comes the part that will amaze and surprise you," said Julie, resuming her carnival voice. "The egg glop drips through the strainer into this mixing bowl with milk and salt and pepper, or whatever you like in it. You can put pancake mix in it if you like, or waffle mix.

"Meanwhile, the force of the egg landing on the strainer releases this carrot in the guinea-pig cage here."

"My guinea pig," interjected Mandy. "His name is Percy."

"Percy sees the carrot and tries to run after it on his treadmill. The treadmill turns the eggbeaters here, which beat up the egg and milk. You see—scrambled eggs! At the same time, the treadmill also winds up this rubber band attached to this wooden arm that holds the bowl, and when it gets too tight"—here she paused, waiting for the rubber band to stretch—"it snaps! Like

164

that! And the arm pivots like so, dumping the contents of the bowl into this frying pan underneath it here.

"The other end of the wooden arm has a piece of flint attached to it which now smashes into this piece of flint here—"

"My flint—" said Jimmy.

"—causing a spark, which ignites this can of Sterno cooking fuel under the frying pan. The eggs start to cook." Julie turned to the crowd. *"Isn't that amazing?"* she said in her best cable TV infomercial voice. And the crowd responded—clapping and cheering— just like an infomercial crowd.

"Cool!" said a student from Mr. Farley's class.

"Shut up," hissed another student from the same class.

"A fire hazard," objected Mr. Lister. "Do they have a fire permit for this?"

"But what about the waking-up part?" asked a judge. "You said it woke you up nicely in time for breakfast."

Julie held up her hands dramatically. Silence fell on the crowd.

"Patience," said Julie. "All will be made clear. Keep your eyes on this string here."

Everyone watched as the flame of the Sterno lit a piece of string strung between the flame and the frying pan. Suddenly, the string hissed into life—it was actually a rocket fuse—and burned slowly until it ignited a little plastic rocket ship balanced on the low end of a small seesaw. The rocket flew straight up into the air, opened a parachute, and floated gently to the ground.

"The rocket ship is not important," said Julie in a

voice that sounded now exactly like the Wizard in *The Wizard of Oz*. "What's important is this." And she gestured to a machine behind the rocket-launching pad—a CD player that suddenly whirred into life.

"You see before you an example of the miracle of infrared light technology at work," explained Julie. "Yes, the high end of the seesaw was blocking the beam from this remote-control device here, which is aimed at the on/off switch of the CD player back there. And so, just at the precise moment when your eggs, your farm-fresh guinea-hen and parrot scrambled eggs super-de-dooper, when they're done cooking, the rocket ship takes off, the end of the seesaw drops down, and the remote beam now strikes the CD player behind it and turns it on. And"—there was a blast of ear-splitting rock and roll from a speaker next to the table Mario was lying on— "your favorite music is piped upstairs to a speaker in your bedroom, gently waking you just in time for breakfast."

Mario, who had either genuinely fallen asleep or done a perfect imitation of it, was now jolted awake with such force that he fell off the table onto the floor. He stumbled to his feet, rubbing his eyes, and the audience burst into laughter.

Julie turned to the crowd and, with perfect timing, concluded: "Ladies and gentlemen, I give you the world's first, the one and only Mighty Muculent Egg-Breaking and Breakfast-Making Morning-Waking Machine!" She took a sweeping bow and the entire room erupted into applause.

"Yes," said Mr. Farley, clapping very slowly and look-

ing all around to see who might agree with him. "Yes, but is it science?"

The superintendent of schools, handing out awards at the end of the day, seemed to think so. Giving the first-place trophy to Mrs. Maxwell's class, he said he found the project "unique" and "original" and "unorthodox" as well as "highly practical." "When can I buy one?" he asked.

So, too, did the cheering parents and the two beaming members of the school board. "You did us proud today, Herbie," said one school-board member, slapping Mr. Bickle on the back. "You did the school proud."

Mr. Bickle smiled shyly. "Well, it was really . . . Mrs. Maxwell is the one who . . . and of course the children are, too."

"Don't be so modest, Herbie." The other school-board member turned to Mr. Lister, who was trying to edge away from them unnoticed.

"There you are, Otis," he boomed. "What do you say to that, eh? Stroke of genius, hiring that woman, on such short notice, too. Don't you agree? Eh?"

"Oh, yes," said Mr. Lister with a nervous laugh. "Genius. It is a pleasure and a privilege to work for such a man as Mr. Bickle."

After the ceremony Simon and Julie slipped away to look for Henrietta. They found her sitting under the table in her box, next to Runcible's cage, as if she'd never left. While Julie picked up the guinea hen to see

if she was okay, Simon opened Runcible's cage and let her sidestep up to his shoulder, where she sat, nibbling his ear and cooing affectionately.

"They must have returned Henny while we were up there getting our award," he said.

Julie looked at Simon and Runcible for a while. "You two look like old friends," she said.

Simon stroked Runcible. "We are," he said.

"Why didn't you say something, about her being your aunt and all?"

"I don't know. I wanted to, but the first day, it was too weird. I felt embarrassed. And then, the longer I waited, the harder it got."

Julie nodded. "Yeah," she said. "I can see that. So what changed your mind?"

"I kept thinking about what you said this morning, about believing in something, no matter how weird it looks to other people."

Once again Julie nodded. She was being unusually quiet. Then she said, in her typical, blunt way, "So what are you going to do about it? To make it up to her, I mean. You must feel pretty rotten. She doesn't know you told everyone just now."

"What *can* I do?" asked Simon miserably. "Stand up in front of the class? And what do I say?"

Julie was silent. She shrugged. It was Runcible, as usual, who piped up.

"Say thank you," said the parrot. "Say you're sorry." She tugged on Simon's hair with her beak. "Get over it."

Badinage

Monday morning. Matilda was late. Simon was writing on the blackboard, and the others were standing around, watching him and talking animatedly.

"They can't fire her now, can they?" said Mindy. "Not after winning the Science Fair."

"Yeah," said Mollie. "We gotta go to the States."

Ethan shrugged. "Hey, I'm just telling you what I heard some of Mr. Farley's kids saying. Grown-ups can do anything they want. It doesn't have to make sense."

Simon interrupted. "Let's try it one more time," he said, pointing to the board. But at that moment the door opened and Jimmy dragged Raggie back into the classroom. Raggie had been standing guard for Mrs. Maxwell, and Jimmy had been standing guard over Raggie. "She's coming!" cried Raggie. Simon looked out the door. In the corridor he could see Mrs. Maxwell and Mr. Lister, deep in conversation. Everyone else ran to their seats.

When Matilda opened the door, the room was completely quiet. The students rose slowly to their feet. They

stood there, all grinning and looking expectantly at her.

She placed Runcible's cage on the floor and went to her desk. The students remained standing. Simon stayed put. Matilda looked at them quizzically.

"Good morning," she said, at last. "And how does your corporosity seem to gashiate today?" She began to delve into her purse.

There was a pause, then, at a signal from Simon, everyone answered in unison:

"*Very discombobulate. Great congruity. Dissimilarity.*"

And then they sat down.

Matilda looked from Simon to the students, and back to Simon. A smile creased her face.

"Thank you, class. You may sit down now, Simon."

"Yes, Aunt Mattie," he said.

170

She smiled again at the words *Aunt Mattie*. Then she addressed Julie.

"By the way, my dear," she said, "it's *corporosity*."

"Huh?" said Julie.

"*Corporosity*. Not *porporosity*: 'How does your *corporosity* seem to *gashiate*.'"

"Oh," said Julie. "Right. *Corporosity*."

There was a silence. Then Jimmy stood up. "Mrs. Maxwell?" he said.

"Yes, dear?"

"They aren't really going to fire you, are they?"

Matilda looked around the classroom again. She looked at the front of the room, where the students had strung all their blue ribbons across the blackboard. She looked at the words Simon had written there: "very discombobulate, great congruity, dissimilarity." She looked at Simon.

"I am glad to see that you have learned *something* from my time here," she said, ignoring the question. And Simon couldn't tell if she was talking to the class, or just to him. "One might even say we had spent our time most—"

"Proficuously?" interjected Raggie.

Matilda smiled. "Precisely. I couldn't have put it better myself. But enough badinage. We have important work to do. After all, we are going to the State Science Fair."

The children cheered. And then from her pockets she produced the familiar porcupine quill, parrot feather, and magnifying glass. "Now children," said Matilda, "the quill—"

"What? You don't know what a whiffet is? Tarnation! What are they teaching you kids, anyway?"

Uncle Philbert's glossary

badinage: joking talk, banter

cabotinage: hamming it up for dramatic effect

jackanape: saucy or mischievous child

miscreant: someone who behaves badly; a criminal

muculent: slimy

nefarious: wicked

pecksniffian: selfish and corrupt while trying to seem friendly and kind

persiflage: lying

proficuous: profitable, useful

quisling: traitor

rodomontade: a bragging, vain, or boastful speech

whiffet: small, young, or unimportant person